The Dragon and the Tiger

"THE FRUIT OF A
WELL-LIVED LIFE
SPRINGS FROM THE
SEED OF GOOD
CONDUCT.
AND THAT IS
KEEPING IN THE
FLOW OF THE DAO."

Master Bao

The Dragon and the Tiger

Master Bao, the Daoist Monk,
and his pupil, Ping, continue their journeys
through China during the T'ang Dynasty
(608 – 917 CE)

By Tom Hanratty

*Thanks to Ellen for her love,
kindness, and gentle support,
over the decades.*

… A Soul like no other.

Table of Contents

The Dragon and the Tiger   1

The Three Paths   13

The Nature of Truth   19

The Lessons of Power   27

The Running Man   33

Woman with the Loaded Sleeves   39

Fear and the Power of Stillness   43

The Dao of Change   47

Ping's Lesson of Respect   55

The Demon of HuShi   61

The Joy of the Present   69

The Poet of the Bamboo Grove   75

The Poisoned Boy   81

The Third Princess   85

The Will of Heaven   95

The Vanishing Gold   101

The Magistrate and the Monk   111

The Water Buffalo and the Dao   117

The Nature of the Snake and the Tiger   121

The Thief   125

    About the Author   133

The Dragon and the Tiger

"A story is a powerful tool, Student Ping...
for creation or destruction."

Master Bao rode his great ox, Xi, along a road that led to the capitol city of Chang'an, in the Shannanxi province. His pupil, Ping, walked alongside.

"I have never seen so many people in one place before, Master," Ping said. "And we haven't even arrived at the South Gate of the city."

"Yes, Ping. This is called The Million-Man City by many. The palaces of the last eight dynasties have been located here, so we'll be seeing many soldiers who guard the emperor."

At the gate, they were stopped briefly by the guards while they registered, but soon were into a street teeming with people.

Crowds surrounded the vendors' stalls that lined both sides of the wide main road. People were purchasing brightly colored scarves and robes, summer fruit and vegetables. Ping wrinkled his nose at the smell of smoked duck and roast pork that seemed to fill the air.

When twelve mounted soldiers trotted past, the gleam of the sun reflecting off their shiny bronze armor, Ping's eyes opened wide. The purple plumes on their helmets and their heavy swords told the citizens these were house guards of the Imperial Palace. The way was immediately cleared for them.

Master Bao, who had a long history with the Dragon Throne, wondered what brought the guards into the city, away from the Imperial Palace where they normally stayed. An important minister or member of the royal family must be in danger, for only the Emperor himself could dispatch a part of his personal force.

"We will stay at *The Inn of Travelers Rest*, Ping. It's in the next street."

After stabling Xi and checking in, the two were shown to a table in the restaurant that was part of the inn. The travelers enjoyed a meal of steamed vegetables and flavorful rice, and welcomed a pot of tea silently served.

Just as the waiter poured a cup for Master Bao,

three heavily armed men strode into the lobby of the inn. The tallest spoke briefly with the clerk, then the three made their way to Master Bao and Ping's table.

Ping immediately jumped to his feet, then fell to his knees with his forehead on the floor, for the men's helmets carried the purple plume of the Imperial House.

All other patrons in the restaurant also dropped to the floor in a full kowtow.

Master Bao remained seated drinking his tea.

The tall leader nodded and the two other guards then took up positions on either side of the door to the lobby.

"Master Bao," the leader said, "I am Colonel Ba Chen of the Imperial Guard. I have orders to bring you with me."

"Who issued those orders, Colonel?"

"The Royal Physician, Dr. Liu Guo. He said I should make it a request."

"An order is hardly a request, Colonel Ba."

Colonel Ba took a deep breath. "Please accompany me, Monk. I have a carriage just outside the door."

"I would like to know my destination, if that is covered in your request."

The officer barked a quick order and the restaurant emptied of all customers except Ping. "We will be going to the home of Governor Pan Fa, one of the

Emperor's most trusted advisors."

Master Bao stood up. "Of course, we will go with you. If someone is in need, it is my duty to help." He bent and put his hand on Ping's back. "Ping, up on your feet. We have a carriage waiting."

It was nearly an hour later when the carriage, accompanied by the twelve Imperial guards, arrived at the inner courtyard of the large home of Governor Pan Fa.

Four men dressed in fine silk met the carriage, their hands clasped in front of them. One, with a long beard of gray and black, stepped forward and bowed to Master Bao.

"I, Dr. Liu Guo, am honored to receive so wise a monk. We heard of your arrival moments after you registered at the South Gate. These men are also physicians, all famous for their healing abilities." All of the men bowed to Master Bao.

Master Bao gave a nod to each man, then said, "What type of disease has struck Governor Pan so that such an illustrious group of physicians needs the help of a poor monk? Perhaps you can give me some particulars, Dr. Liu."

"Two weeks ago," began Dr. Liu, "Governor Pan was a healthy fifty year old advisor to the Emperor. Suddenly, without warning, he began to become weaker and weaker. I, myself, and all the most prominent doctors tried herbs, acupuncture, and other healing techniques known only to a few monks. Nothing worked. Now, the Governor is unable to sit up, or even talk. He seems conscious most of the time, but is fading rapidly. His *Qi* is leaving his body and we don't believe he will live more than a day or two.

"Governor Pan's first wife died two years ago, and last year he married his former concubine. The young woman is devoted to him, and sits at his bedside all day."

"If none of your ministrations have worked," Master Bao said, "it must indeed be a formidable illness."

"It is not an illness of this earth, Master Bao. He has been struck with an evil spell, sent by the magician Wang Ho. A tiger's tooth was found under his headrest on the morning he became ill."

"Why do you suspect Wang Ho? Surely, a man as prominent as Governor Pan would have many enemies."

"Wang Ho, who was known for his Tiger Power, threatened the Governor after he found Wang guilty of being a were-tiger, a beheading offence, as you know. Wang swore revenge as the sentence was pronounced," one of the other physicians said.

"So if Wang is gone, who put the tiger's tooth under the headrest?"

"The ghost of Wang, of course," said a second

doctor. "Wang was captured as he changed from a tiger into a man, after a night of horrific violence."

"Did the Governor have any visitors from outside the home before he became ill?"

"Just his step-son, who is a hunter. It was he who caught the Weretiger Wang. He lives in a far part of the city and, as is his filial duty, visits the Governor each month."

"Very well," Master Bao responded. "What is it you wish me to do?"

"Break the spell that is killing the Governor," Dr. Liu said.

"Then I will need twelve candles, fifteen incense sticks, and the wing of a hawk."

The doctors departed after leading Master Bao and Ping to a large room lined with bookshelves.

Ping, who had listened carefully to all that was said, bowed deeply before the monk, his hands clasped in his capacious sleeves. "Can a true *Follower of the Way* fight such a powerful evil?" he whispered. "Perhaps the ghost of Wang will be angry if we interfere."

Master Bao smiled. "Evil and Good are constructs of people for actions and events. To the *Followers of the Dao*, Student Ping, they are simply names, for the *Dao* does not see Evil or Good.

"The *Dao*, like the mountain stream, nourishes equally both the lady of virtue and the murderous bandit. And ghosts have other matters to attend to in the Spirit World. They don't have time or interest in bothering us.

"No, Ping. There is something very much of this world at play here."

In a short time, Master Bao and Ping were led to a large bedroom where Governor Pan lay on his back. A beautiful young woman sat next to his bed. She looked up when the men entered the room, and began to weep softly. One of the doctors called a handmaiden to accompany the distressed lady to the women's quarters.

The four doctors carried the twelve candles and fifteen incense sticks into the room, then stood aside. Ping lit the candles and Master Bao ignited the incense after arranging them around the Governor. The curtains were drawn so the room was darkened, but for the soft glow of the candles. The air was redolent of incense.

Then Master Bao examined the Governor, noting his pale complexion, the darkened circles under his eyes, and his dry skin. The nine pulses in each wrist felt like a thin thread under the monk's fingers, with a very slow beat. Checking the Governor's tongue, eyes, and body for signs of poisoning, Master Bao found none.

When Master Bao began to whisper to the Governor while slowly fanning the patient with the hawk wing, the royal doctors looked at each other and shook their heads. This was a treatment they had never before seen.

A few minutes later, Governor Pan's eyes popped open, and a smile played across his lips. The doctors hurried to his bedside and helped him sit up. A cup of wine was put in his hand, and one of the physicians ran to get some food for the patient.

The spell was broken.

When the physicians turned to thank the monk, they found the room empty. Master Bao and Ping, their task finished, had left.

Later that day at the inn, Master Bao and Ping had just finished their evening rice when Colonel Ba Chen entered the restaurant. This time, he was dressed in civilian clothing, with no insignia to proclaim his position in the army.

Master Bao and Ping both rose and offered the Colonel a seat at their table. After tea had been poured for all three, the Colonel smiled at the monk.

"Master Bao. We are grateful for your healing of the Governor, but there are two questions that have been bothering me. Who put the tiger's tooth under the headrest of the Governor? And who cast the evil spell?"

"I can't answer those questions, Colonel, because I

have no knowledge of the actions of the people closest to Governor Pan Fa before his illness."

Colonel Ba nodded. "I understand your reluctance to accuse anyone, but the Governor's life was in danger, and I am asking for any help in meeting future threats. From your knowledge of evil spells and human nature, I wish you to agree or disagree with what I am about to tell you."

Master Bao was quiet for a long moment." What would you require of me?"

"A simple nod will do, Monk, to tell me if I'm moving in the right direction."

"What are your thoughts, Colonel?"

"I have one of my spies following the Governor's young wife. And have another following his step-son, a handsome man near the wife's age, who is a hunter and has access to the teeth of tigers."

Master Bao nodded.

Without another word, Colonel Ba left the restaurant.

Ping watched the departing soldier with his head tilted to one side. He poured another cup of tea, then rose and bowed to the monk.

"Master, this pupil is perplexed. How was the evil spell cast, and how did you break the spell? Please enlighten this ignorant student."

Master Bao took sip of tea, then smiled. "It is easy

to break a spell when there is no spell, Ping. I suspect someone took advantage of Wang Ho's threat and used it to poison the mind of the Governor. Perhaps a drug was used to soften his rational mind, and open it to suggestion. Over a period of weeks, he was daily told a story until he began to believe the lies about the spell. Then, finally, the tiger's tooth pushed him into thinking he was dying. The power of suggestion, Ping, can be strong even in a man like Governor Pan."

"What of the candles and incense, Master? How did they help heal the Governor?"

"Much like in stage plays, Student Ping, the atmosphere is important to trick the mind into believing something mysterious is happening. The flickering candles cast moving shadows, and the odor of the incense added the subtle atmosphere of spiritual events. They helped me enter the deep layers of the Governor's mind where his fears and doubts were holding his rational mind hostage."

"But you only waved a hawk wing over him and talked," Ping said.

"He was believing a false story, Ping. I told him another, of a tiger being swallowed by a dragon.

"The hawk wing moved the air over his skin, and it helped open up his *Qi meridians*. I told him it was the breath of the dragon. His rational mind then made the connection to the power of the Dragon Throne, throwing off the bonds of fear and doubt.

"A story is a powerful tool, Student Ping, for creation or destruction. It can implant a belief. And that belief can either block or enhance the flow of *Qi*, the life force of the body. I simply changed the story, opened up his *Qi meridians*, and his own mind did the rest."

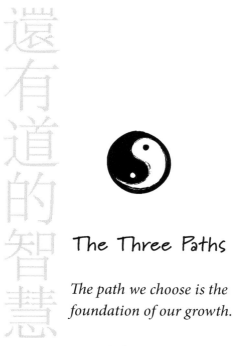

The Three Paths

The path we choose is the foundation of our growth.

Master Bao rode his ox, Xi, along a country trail in the Providence of Wei. His student, Ping, walked alongside.

"We will soon come to a place where the road branches, Ping. I want you to think deeply about each path before we continue our journey."

An hour later, the trail split into three roads.

A large sign said the wide boulevard to the left led to Jing Shi.

"Jing Shi is a city of commerce, student Ping. It is located on a busy canal that connects two major rivers. It is said the sun never sets on Jing Shi, for the parties in the large houses go all night. The Willow Quarter is busy all hours of the day, and the Courtesans are noted for their singing and creative abilities. Expensive wines are brought by the ships using the canal, and goods from around the Empire are available to purchase."

Student Ping simply nodded.

"This middle road," the monk went on, "while not as wide as the one to Jing Shi, is of packed earth, with colorful flowers along its edge. It leads to the town of Chi Zhen. Master craftsmen live in this town, and some of the most beautiful silk cloth with exquisite embroidery is found here. Both men and women are hard-working, honest and happy. The fields surrounding Chi Zhen are fertile with grain, and its rice paddies are bountiful."

Student Ping simply nodded.

The road to the right was really a dirt trail, boarded by tall trees, and appeared little used. Grass sprouted between cart tracks.

"Where does this third track lead, Master?" Ping asked.

"This is the beginning of the trail that leads to the *Shen Monastery of the White Clouds*. It lies in the mountains," Master Bao responded.

Ping folded his hands into his capacious sleeves, raised his hands to eye level, and bowed. "Master, please inform this ignorant pupil. Is there something else I should know about these three roads?"

"Yes, Ping. The first road, to Jing Shi, is wide, well-tended, but it is very long for the traveler. It favors those with wealth enough to own a horse or a palanquin."

Ping simply nodded.

"The second road, to Chi Zhen, is more difficult. It is also long and is mostly up a steep grade. It is a hard path, with a few obstructions, but leads to a place of happiness and satisfaction for most."

Ping nodded. "And the third, Master? The one to the monastery?"

"That is the most difficult of all, Student Ping. It's a long, rocky, mountain trail beset by hardship, danger from the cold, and cruel bandits who lie in wait. Only the strong will arrive at the *Shen Monastery of the White Clouds*. Others will turn back.

"Once there, however, the kindly monks will provide a safe and peaceful home for the weary traveler. The pilgrim will drink from the clear mountain stream which is said to refresh above all others, and eat fresh food from the gardens tended by the monks. The traveler will need to carry water and chop wood to help maintain the monastery, but equanimity, peace, and understanding of life is possible at this monastery in the clouds."

Ping smiled and nodded.

"Remember, the path we choose becomes the

foundation of our growth from body, to energy, to spirit," said Master Bao."

Ping smiled and nodded,

"Which path do we take, Student Ping?"

Ping thought for a long time, then bowed again tomorrow.

"I have seen little of the world, Master, and am ignorant of most things. Only an Enlightened Master such as yourself can answer so important a question."

Master Bao smiled. "You have grown in wisdom, Ping. The difficult path to the *Shen Monastery of the White Clouds* is the way we will someday take.

"But today, let us travel the road to Jing Shi, and see what we can learn. There are many lessons for us among people who are concerned only with wealth, power, and comfort. The inhabitants of this city are entangled in their bodies' energies.

"Later, we will travel to Chi Zhen, for lessons of hard work and satisfaction. The people of this town are happy with their lot in this life. They will teach us much about living with our heart energies.

"Finally, Ping, we will take the difficult path to enlightenment and equanimity. The *Shen Monastery of White Clouds* is closest to the *Dao*.

"It is there, embracing the *essence* of the spirit of the natural world, we will learn the lessons of truly becoming *One with the Dao*."

"And from there, Master?" Ping asked.

"We then travel back to help others, and wait on the *Will of Heaven* to guide us."

The Nature of Truth

*Ping learns the difference between
Truth and Reality.*

Master Bao rode his great ox, Xi, along a road
leading to the market town of Mai Hui in
the province of Huainan. His student, Ping, walked
alongside.

"Master, I have heard Mai Hui is a wealthy town
on a great canal. Will we be staying at an inn there?"

"Yes, Ping," Master Bao replied, "We will stop at
The Inn of Quiet Repose that has a restaurant well-
known for its fine Jasmine rice and roasted vegetables. Tomorrow, we will move on to the Monastery
where we will meet with some of the *Immortals*."

"Oh Master, how can I, an ignorant student, speak
with men and women who have lived nearly 150 years,

and are renowned for their knowledge of life? These great people will soon be in the clouds with the Jade Emperor."

Master Bao laughed. "Don't worry, Ping. You have ideas and thoughts known only to you, and this will give you a chance to share them with some of the wisest people in the Empire. They are always happy to hear new ways of seeing the world through fresh eyes."

The travelers registered at the inn, stabled Xi in the barn, and went for a walk through the market-place of the village. The vendors in the crowded street were selling everything from silk scarves to fruits and vegetables. Ping inhaled the pleasant smell of smoked duck and roasted pork.

"This village is a crossroads for canal traffic, and is the main road to the capitol of the province, Ping. People from throughout the Empire and foreign coun-tries visit Mai Hui."

As Ping and Master Bao were conversing with a vendor of rice cakes, a man ran quickly past. Sec-onds later, the shout of "Thief," split the air, and a heavyset man, dressed in the leather vest and cap of the village warden, puffed up the street. Suddenly, he stopped, bent over, and put his hands on his knees, as he gasped for air.

"Did anyone see the thief?" he shouted when he regained his breath. "He stole a string of pearls from the goldsmith Wang. Can anyone tell me what he looked like? I only caught a glimpse of him, he ran so fast."

"I'm Lu Chien," a wealthy merchant said, as he stepped from the crowd. "I saw him clearly. He was dressed as a beggar, in rags, and had a yellow band tied around his head. I think he had a scar on his face. A typical thug."

The warden smiled and nodded.

"No, no. That's not how he looked at all," said another man. "I'm Ma, an artisan. The man was dressed in red and white silk robes and had a small green turban on his head. Obviously, a Barbarian."

"That's not it at all," said a third man, pushing his way to the front of the crowd. "I'm Fa Hua, a vegetable farmer. The man was very tall, had a black shirt and brown pants, with straw sandals on his feet. He looked angry, with a scowl on his face."

"You're all wrong." A fourth man stepped to the front of the crowd. "I'm Yi Da, the baker, here in the market selling my rice cakes. The man was dressed in fine silk robes of purple. He was short and thin. and had a beard, neatly trimmed. Obviously, a rich young man looking for trouble."

The warden threw up his arms, turned and stomped away, shaking his head.

Later, when the monk and Ping were eating their

evening rice at the restaurant of *The Inn of Quiet Repose*, Ping stood and bowed deeply, his hands clasped inside his capacious sleeves.

"Master, how can so many people describe the thief so differently," Ping asked. "What is the truth? What did the man really look like, and how was he dressed?"

Master Bao sipped his tea. "Please sit, Student Ping. There is an important lesson in all this. Perhaps more then one."

After Ping sat down, Master Bao continued. "You have just seen the difference between truth and reality.

"Each of the witnesses who saw the thief were looking through several layers or veils. We view the world and events through veils of our own history.

"Let me give examples of each. I will not list the veils for each man, but be assured they were there.

"The first layer was what they expected to see in a thief.

"For example, the wealthy merchant, Mr. Lu, saw a poor man, because to him, it is poor people who are criminals. He then gave the thief the clothing of a poor man, and a headband a rebel would wear. He even saw a scar on the face of the thief, because he would expect a poor thief to have a scar. This is Mr. Lu's reality, Ping.

"The second layer the witnesses looked through

was their own prejudices.

"The artisan, Mr. Ma, saw a Barbarian. So he saw red and white silk robes and a green turban as a foreigner from the Arabian countries would wear. To Mr. Ma, all criminals are probably Barbarians, and all Barbarians are likely criminals.

"The third veil the witness looked through was with whom they are familiar, the people they know well, such as their neighbors or friends.

"The farmer, Mr. Fa, is rather short, so he saw a tall man, dressed in the black shirt and brown pants of a farmer, with straw sandals, common footwear for farmers.

"The fourth veil is the mist of gossip, family teachings about people, and conversation heard when friends get together.

"For this veil, we will look at the baker, Mr. Yi. He has probably heard of the reckless youth of the wealthy class, the gossip and recriminations for a group of people he really knows nothing about. In his ignorance, he has filled in thoughts and complaints from other bakers. The purple robes are expensive, and the well trimmed beard is common to young men of that class."

Ping thought for a long moment. "Then, Master, all these men lied?"

"No, Ping. They reported what they saw. But each

was looking though their personal veils.

"We see with our minds, Ping, as well as with our eyes."

"Then what is truth, Master, if we can't believe our eyes?"

"Truth is absolute. Reality is different for each person," Master Bao said, "and when many people are involved, it is often easier to discover the truth from facts.

"Facts are truth in small pieces.

"In this case, I saw that the thief stepped in a puddle of water. His track showed he was barefooted, and, from the size of the print, about as tall as me."

"He caught his sleeve on the nail of the melon vendor's cart as he ran past. The piece of cloth he left behind showed he was dressed in a blue wool robe.

"After he fled around the corner, I found he had dropped a scarf of blue silk, that, when he ran past, was wrapped around the lower part of his face. Mr. Lu, Mr. Fa, and Mr. Yi all reported seeing the thief's face, but all they saw was what they expected a thief to look like."

"Master, are you going to tell the Warden what you have learned?"

Master Bao took a deep breath. "In back of you, in a corner of this restaurant, behind a gauze screen, is the very man I described. Sitting with him is the

Warden, who is closely examining a string of pearls. You perhaps noticed the cry of "Thief," was not shouted until the young man had run past."

Ping slowly turned and peered through the gauze curtain.

"I think what I have learned is already known to the Warden."

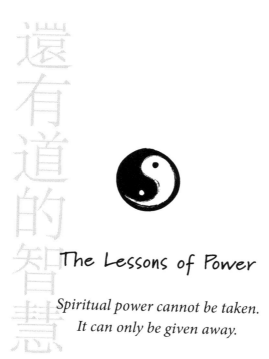

The Lessons of Power

Spiritual power cannot be taken.
It can only be given away.

Master Bao rode his ox, Xi, along a wide, well-traveled road in the kingdom of Hwang-Liu. His pupil, Ping, walked alongside.

"Soon, Ping, we will be in the city of Peng-ho, the capitol of this kingdom. Since this is the Fifth day of the Fifth Moon, the date of the annual Dragon Boat Festival, we may need to sleep in one of the huts that are provided for the farmers and merchants coming from all over Hwang-Liu. All the inns will be filled."

Ping was smiling broadly. "I saw a Dragon Boat race once, Master, when I was still at home. I have heard the ones on the River Chu in Peng-ho are wondrous to behold, eighty rowers in each Dragon Boat."

"Yes, Ping. It is a great holiday for our hardworking people. It gives them a chance to eat traditional filled rice cakes and place bets on their favorite crew. It is rumored the Prince of Hwang-Liu will be giving away the prizes to the winning crew."

"I have never seen a prince, Master, nor any member of a royal family."

Master Bao smiled. "Perhaps today you will."

An hour later, the travelers entered the gates of Peng-ho, found a stable for Xi, and a hut for themselves. The huts, canvas tents, had been erected to house the overflow of festival-goers.

"Come, Ping. The sun has set and the starting gong has sounded. Cheers from the crowd tell us the boats are coming into sight around the bend in the river. We can see the finish line from that knoll near the Prince's floating palace. Ordinary citizens are not allowed near the Prince's boat, but I'm sure the guards will not object to an old monk and his student standing quietly by."

After a quick glance, the heavily armed guards ignored the monk and Ping, and instead watched the large Dragon boats as they flew across the finish line.

The Prince of Hwang-Liu, a young man with no beard or mustache, sat on his throne which was covered in gold, in the stern of the floating palace. His brocade robe was elaborately embroidered and had wide gold sleeves. His black hat was trimmed in red. A man with a gray beard was on his right, bent double in a low bow. Other men were gathered around the throne, all either bowing deeply or kneeling. One man, however, tall and covered in bright armor, stood behind the throne, torch light shining off his golden helmet.

Master Bao, who had known many kings and princes, kept an eye on Ping. The glitter of the trappings and the obeisance of the men surrounding the prince seemed to hold Ping in awe. When the prince turned toward the monk and Ping, the student dropped to his knees and knocked his forehead on the ground three times.

Master Bao merely gazed back at the monarch, who yawned and looked away.

Later, after the last boat had crossed the finish line and the Prince had handed out the prizes to the winners, Master Bao and Ping took their evening rice at a small restaurant on a side street.

After their simple meal, Ping stood and, his hands clasped inside his capacious sleeves, gave a deep bow. "Master, please enlighten this ignorant student. It is known that the common people must kneel in the presence of the royal family.

"But the men surrounding the Prince today were men of stature, with rich robes and hats. They had their own servants and palanquins. Why were they kneeling and bowing?"

"One word, Ping. Power." the monk replied.

"I see power in the thunder and lightening," Ping said. "There is power in the plants who grow despite the rocks, and the streams in the mountains pour forth power as they tumble down the slope."

Master Bao thought for a long moment. "All things in this Universe, including humans, are given power, but some see only the power outside themselves. They trade the power within for the power without, and see the Prince as the source of that power."

"What, then, is power, Master? The Prince can have a man beheaded. Is that power?"

"Yes. He has the power to destroy, and that is a great power. History teaches us that it must be wielded with restraint, however, or he will lose the *Mandate of Heaven* and be destroyed himself.

"As a wise monarch, then, he uses his power to get others to do his bidding. For example, the Minister of Finance, who was the elderly man standing next to the throne, knows the Prince can reward him, so he bows to curry favor. This is known as reward power.

"The leader of the Goldworker's Guild was also with the Prince, and he fears the Prince will withdraw his support of the gold prices, so he bows and kneels. This is known as threatening power.

"Behind the throne stood General Hong, the head of the Army. He respects the *Mandate of Heaven* and therefore the Prince's authority as the legal ruler. He, among those men, will remain loyal. This is known as legitimate power."

Ping bowed again. "The Prince could have had you beheaded for not kneeling. Why did he not use that power?"

"Because he recognized that is just the power over my body, not my spirit. He is wise, for he knows he cannot have my compliance by force. Therefore, he did not send his soldiers to arrest me, as would have a more arrogant prince.

"Beheading an elderly monk would not have increased his power, and may have led to an uprising among the People of this kingdom.

"An enlightened monarch knows he cannot take a man or woman's spiritual power by force. Only their physical body."

"How does one then lose their spiritual power?" Ping asked.

"We give it away, Student Ping. Anger, disappointment, or violence is giving away our power to others. If a man insults you and you become angry, you have given him the power to influence how you feel. If you strike another, it is because you have given him the power to push you into disharmony.

"The lesson, Ping, is to hold onto your power by remaining innocent, gentle, and accepting of the *Will of Heaven.*

"But for now, while still a student, it would be wise to kneel when expected."

Thanks to "The Bases of Social Power"
by Raven and French, in Group Dynamics,
Harper and Row, 1959, for the idea.

The Running Man

*Real wealth is peace
of mind.*

Master Bao rode his great ox, Xi, along a high mountain road in the province of Han-Yung. His pupil Ping strode alongside.

"Soon, Ping, we will be in the village of Yuen Chi known for its twin lakes, and bountiful fields of grain."

"With two lakes for fishing and fields of grain, the people of Yuen Chi must be very happy," Ping said.

"Yes, Ping. There is plentiful food. When drought strikes the rest of the province, the water from the lakes is used to irrigate the fields. It is a very content village."

"Will we be stopping at an inn, or sleeping beneath the stars tonight, Master?"

"*The Inn of Quiet Repose* is noted for its vast vegetable garden, as well as its clean rooms. It is there we will spend the night. We should be seeing the twin lakes before too long. The village is set on a strip of land between them."

About an hour later, the road leveled off and ran between two large lakes. Several fishermen in small boats were busy working with their tame cormorants. Soon, the travelers were on Yuen Chi's crowded main street, walking among well-dressed merchants and bare-footed farmers in their simple shirts and pants.

"The people look happy, Master," Ping said, "and I see very few beggars."

Master Bao nodded. "If you notice, several of the buildings have the same name, 'Liu.' Over there is 'Liu's Cotton Goods,' across the street from 'Liu's Leather Shop.'"

"I saw a 'Liu's Goldsmith,' and a 'Liu's Fish Restaurant,'" Ping added

"Whoever Liu is, he must be quite wealthy. But here is *The Inn of Quiet Repose*, and a stable behind it. We'll have the stable hand give Xi a rubdown and feed him, for he's had a long trip today. Then, we'll register in the inn."

In a short time, Master Bao and Ping entered the wide doorway of the inn and approached the registration desk. A tall clerk with a full gray beard greeted the travelers with a bow and a smile.

"Our inn is honored to have two guests such as yourselves," he said. "We have quiet rooms in the courtyard."

A clash and clatter of cymbals and drums erupted from the street outside the inn, and the sound of people shouting filled the lobby. The innkeeper merely smiled, and continued to prepare the registration book.

Ping ran to the door and peered out. "The Magistrate must be approaching," he said over the din. "Or perhaps a member of the Dragon Throne family."

"No, no," the innkeeper answered, "it's just Mr. Liu hurrying past. He doesn't stop here, or really anywhere, for he works day and night. The shouts and noise you hear are his men chasing people out of his way, for he hates to be delayed."

Ping watched as a closed palanquin, carried by six chair-bearers, rushed down the street. A group of drummers ran before them, beating on skin drums, brass cymbals, and iron triangles.

"The story of Mr. Liu is famous throughout this province," the innkeeper revealed. "His father was a prominent fisherman, who owned his own boat. So Liu knew hard work, but also comfort as a child. He was a curious boy, so my old clerk taught him to read and write.

"A tragedy struck, however. One day, Liu's father's boat floundered in a storm and only Liu lived. Soon, poor Liu's mother died of a broken heart. His family gone, the boat gone, Liu was forced to work for other fishermen, and soon was reduced to rags.

"One day, a rich merchant's son jeered at him, calling him names. The next day, people noticed that Liu had disappeared. No one heard from him for three years, but when he returned, he had a gold bar with which he bought a small wine shop. Since then, he has worked night and day to expand his holdings. Now, as a young man of only thirty, he is far richer than the merchant's son who drove him away."

That evening, as Master Bao and Ping were finishing their evening rice with fresh vegetables in the restaurant in the inn, the sound of shouting came from the lobby.

"Mr. Liu is dead," a man screamed. "He just dropped over while at his desk." The restaurant patrons, except for Master Bao and Ping, rushed out into the street.

Ping studied the monk's face, waiting for a reaction. After several minutes, Ping said, "What do you think happened, Master?"

Master Bao seemed to be examining the teapot sitting between the two. "The local Magistrate will no doubt order an examination by the Coroner, but I think he will find that Mr. Liu simply stopped running."

Ping rose and bowed deeply to , his hands clasped inside his capacious sleeves. "Please enlighten this ignorant student, Master. Mr. Liu was not running. He was at his desk."

Master Bao smiled. "Our wise Zhuangzi once told a story about a running man.

"There once lived a man who feared his own shadow. This man also feared the sound of his own footsteps.

"So the man ran and ran, but unable to outrun his own shadow and the sound of his footsteps, he finally dropped dead from running."

The monk filled both teacups. "Do you find a lesson in this story, Student Ping, that may help understand Mr. Liu?"

Ping smiled broadly. "If the man had stopped running, he would no longer hear his footsteps. Perhaps Mr. Liu feared his past was catching up with him."

"And?" Master Bao inquired.

Ping thought for a moment. "And, if he sat in the shade of a tree, he would not see his shadow. Do you think, Master, that Mr. Liu feared poverty, as this man in the story feared his shadow?"

"Perhaps. Real wealth, as *Followers of the Way* know, is peace of mind, brought about by equanimity.

"And remember, Student Ping, equanimity does not come from running away from one's fears."

Thanks to Zhuangzi
(369 – 286 BCE) for the idea

Woman with the Loaded Sleeves

*Desire is the nourishment
that does not nourish.*

O
n a warm spring day, Master Bao and his student, Ping, walked along the city streets of Jing Lai, in the province of Guannei, known for its "Willow and Flower" district.

Ping had been watching the elegant young women, dressed in colorful flowing robes, fanning themselves on the balconies of the Flower Halls.

"The *Dao* is the natural way of life, young Ping," Master Bao said, with one eye on his student. "It is the natural flow of the Universe."

"Yes, Master," Ping replied, "But my whole body responds to the presence of these beautiful girls. I greatly desire to be in their presence. Is that not also in the flow of the Universe?"

Master Bao smiled. "All things are in the *Flow of the Dao*, and your desire is a passion known to all humans. In the young, it is the fire at the foot of the mountain."

The travelers arrived at a two-story restaurant with a sign proclaiming it to be *The Rice Bowl of the Gods*. After sitting at a table near the back, Master Bao continued, "In the spring, the life force in all things stirs again, and this is what you are feeling now. But beware that your desire is not the nourishment that does not nourish."

Ping bowed his head. "Please inform this ignorant student about the dangers of desire, Master."

Before Master Bao could respond, the waiter brought large bowls of noodles and a pot of tea, and the two ate with gusto. After they were finished, Ping filled their teacups.

Just then, a young woman entered the restaurant. On her arm, a man with a long white beard, nearly bent double, shuffled beside her. As they moved toward a table near the door, their way was blocked by a large man with a ring beard and a sneer that showed darkened teeth. He had risen from a nearby table where three other men were sitting.

Master Bao noted all four had the deep chests and sturdy necks of boxers, and were likely "brothers of the green woods," that is, professional criminals.

"Lose this old goat, my beauty, and join me and my friends in a round of fine wine," the thug said as he took the girl's arm.

Ping started to rise from the table, but Master Bao put his hand on Ping's arm. "Wait, Ping. You are about to see a rare sight. Those men are going to get a lesson they won't soon forget."

As the large man began to pull the girl away from the old man, her right sleeve swirled as she spun away. Something in her capacious sleeve struck the thug on the side of his face, turning loose a stream of blood from his mouth. He dropped to the floor holding his jaw.

As his companions came to the man's aid, the girl, with seemingly little effort, whirled her sleeves and shattered first one man's arm, then another's shoulder. The last man dove under the table to escape the mayhem.

The men fled from the restaurant, as the young woman with her elderly companion pulled up chairs and sat at the table. Bowls of noodles and a pot of tea were instantly brought by the waiter.

"Note, Ping," Master Bao said. "The young lady carries a lead ball in each sleeve and has been trained in the ancient art of 'Loaded Sleeve Fighting.' I saw her sleeves were loaded when she entered the room, but the thugs were blinded by their desire."

Ping stood and bowed deeply to the monk. "Master," Ping said, "These men were after that girl for vile reasons. Is this what you meant by 'nourishment that does not nourish?'"

"Yes, Student Ping. The gratification they sought would lead to still more desire, and the mad pursuit of pleasure for base satisfaction of the senses leads to misfortune.

"Proper conduct, with *equanimity*, *gentleness*, and *humility*, will obtain the goal which one seeks. This is a lesson people of any age must learn in order to reach the top of the mountain."

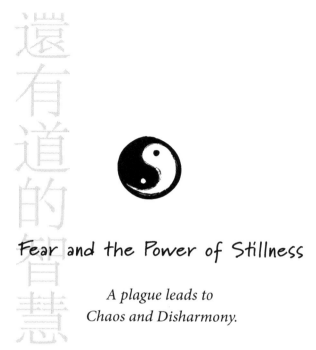

Fear and the Power of Stillness

A plague leads to
Chaos and Disharmony.

"This is a city of fear," Master Bao said, as he looked over the darkening town.

The monk, his student Ping, and the Magistrate stood on the balcony of the Tribunal of the capitol of Wei Gong Prefecture. They watched the sun, a soft blur, as it settled behind the purple mountains that rose near the metropolis, casting the town in deep shadow.

"The Plague has made it a city ruled by the *Spirit of Death*," the Magistrate standing next to the monk said. "I no longer have power to help the people."

Ping gazed up at the starless sky. The low clouds seemed to settle over the city like a stuffy shroud, holding in the moist heat. He felt his thin shirt cling to his body, and thought of standing under an icy mountain waterfall.

The Magistrate gave a deep sigh. "At this hour, the street hawkers should be crying out their final calls for their wares, and the music of the Willow Quarter should be clearly heard. Even the drums and gongs of the Buddhist Temples are silent. But now, it is a city filled with the stench of death and wails of those dying."

"Have you followed my suggestions?" Master Bao asked as he turned to the Magistrate.

"Yes. We have repaired the grates to keep rats out of the city, and have stopped ships from coming into our port. The people don't like having to stay in their houses and covering their faces when out for food; but if it will help, they do so."

Just then, Ping felt a slight breeze on his cheek, and a few large raindrops began to hit his face as he turned it to the sky.

The Magistrate smiled broadly. "The Evil Spell is broken," he shouted. "Now, the plague will be washed away."

And within two weeks, the disease lifted and the Magistrate declared the plague over.

Three weeks later, Master Bao and Ping left the capitol city behind. The monk rode his ox, Xi, and Ping walked alongside.

"The countryside will be dangerous, Ping," Master

Bao said, "for plagues and war create chaos, and chaos in the land breeds disharmony in people."

"And people who are in disharmony are dangerous?" Ping asked.

"Yes, Ping," came the reply. "There are those who are starving and seek food, and those who have lost loved ones and seek solace.

"But the most dangerous ones are those who seek to gain from the chaos. They seek neither food nor solace, but greed drives them to tear apart the fabric of the society. Chaos, for some, offers opportunity for profit."

Just then, a large group of mounted men, banishing swords and spears, roared over a hill, driving toward the monk and Ping, yelling curses.

Ping exclaimed, "Master! What should we do?"

Master Bao smiled and said, "Go to your stillness inside, Ping. Simply accept what the *Will of Heaven* sends us, and you won't be harmed."

Ping closed his eyes and let his mind go blank, as Master Bao had taught him many times. The terror he had felt seemed to melt away to be replaced by a deep, encompassing sense of peace and good will.

As Master Bao and his student remained quietly at rest, the hoard thundered past, flowing around the ox and two travelers as if they were a natural obstruction in their path, like a tree or rock.

After the dust settled, Ping, his hands folded inside his capacious sleeves, approached Master Bao, and bowed deeply.

"Please teach this ignorant pupil, Master, by what power were we spared? Did you work some magic so we became invisible?"

"No, student Ping. "It is the *Great Law of the Dao* that we will be sent lessons we must learn. Whether we are beset by plague or must contend with people who have become filled with anger and hatred, by maintaining our *equilibrium, inner stillness*, and *acceptance*, we will prevail.

"That is the lesson we have been gifted to learn today."

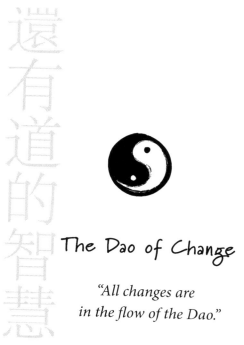

The Dao of Change

*"All changes are
in the flow of the Dao."*

Master Bao rode his great Ox, Xi, along a tract through a thick grove of wide-leaved trees. His pupil, Ping, walked alongside, a large smile on his face.

"Master Bao," Ping said. "These leaves on the trees are red, brown, and golden. They are beautiful, especially where the morning sun strikes them."

The monk smiled back at Ping. "Yes, Ping. And the mist in the forest holds the sunbeams so we can witness an enhanced beauty of Nature."

The two traveled in silence, the only sound the birds on branches, and the crunch of dry leaves under the hoofs of the ox.

"I remember in the winter when the branches were bare," Ping said. "The forest we were traveling through was dark and cold. And in the Spring, the buds turned the forest into a green world, before it became the golden grove of autumn, as it is now."

Master Bao simply smiled and nodded.

THE VILLAGE OF LANCHOW

After about another mile, Master Bao turned to Ping. "We should be in Lanchow Village in another hour, Ping. It was ravaged by war, and has seen some hard times."

Soon, the chirping of the birds and the breeze in the branches were replaced by the deep thump of a large drum.

"Master Bao. That is a funeral drum. It must be coming from Lanchow Village."

Shortly, Master Bao and Ping entered the gate of the Village of Lanchow and made their way to *The Inn of Peaceful Repose*. All through the street, the shops were closed and people stood in groups speaking quietly. Some of the villagers were openly weeping.

After stabling the ox, the two entered the inn. Behind the counter, the innkeeper sat on a tall stool, but his shoulders drooped and he sighed heavily as the two travelers approached his desk.

"You've come on a sad day, Monk. Our village

elder, the kindest man in the Empire, has passed away and his burial is today. The people of the village and the farmers from the land surrounding the town are here to pay their respects. We have only one room with two beds left in the inn, and it is not our best so you can have it at no cost."

"Thank you for your kindness, Innkeeper," Master Bao said. "But tell me about this man who has died. He must have been well liked to receive such an outpouring of grief."

"That he was, Master. He gave food to all who were hungry, clothing to the needy, and shared his wealth with the town. Until his age became heavy on his shoulders, and enfeebled by the passing years, his counsel was sought by rich and poor alike."

The next day, Master Bao and Ping left the village of Lanchow and journeyed into an area rich with fields of grain, and well-tended rice patties.

MASTER BAO EXPLAINS THE CHANGE CALLED DEATH

"Why is death so painful, Master?" Ping asked as they made their way through the land.

"Life and death are both in the *Flow of the Dao*, Ping. It is our human perception of death as an end to existence, rather than just a change, that brings grief."

Pei Lei Village

By evening, Ping noted the land was drier, the fields showing stunted plants and there were hovels for houses.

"Master," Ping asked with a worried glance toward a grove of trees blackened by a long-ago fire, "will we be staying in a village tonight, or sleeping under the stars?"

"The village of Pei Lei is just ahead, Ping. *The Inn of Weary Travelers* is on the main street. It was once the most comfortable place to spend a night. But much has changed in the years since I first visited Pei lei."

The sun had dropped behind the distant dark hills when Master Bao and Ping arrived at *The Inn of Weary Travelers*. The stable was still open and the ox, Xi, was turned over to the stable lad.

A small oil lamp hung over the curtain door to the inn, and, by its dim light, Master Bao pulled the curtain aside and he and Ping entered the small lobby. Behind the counter, a squat, hulking man with a rough ringbeard sat scowling at the travelers. He wore an open dark vest that left his muscled arms and broad hairy chest bare. Two smoky candles on the counter gave the only light. A strong odor of burnt grease filled the air.

"We have no rooms, Monk. But for a string of coppers you and your servant can sleep in the barn with the animals," the man growled. "A bowl of noo-dles goes with the straw, if you're not too particular."

Master Bao gave a slight bow. "Thank you for your kind offer," Master Bao said. "Your price is too high."

As Master Bao and Ping left the inn, they were approached by a lean man holding an oil lantern. He was dressed in a patched coat that had been in style some years past, and his thin face was lined with worry.

"Please excuse the lout in the inn," the man said with a deep bow. "I recognized you from your visit here back when I owned this very inn. Your wisdom and kindness made a great impression on me."

Master Bao responded with a bow. "I greatly enjoyed my stay here."

"This humble person is named Meng Gai, and I invite you and your student to stay at my miserable dwelling. Your presence would be a great honor. It is just a hovel, but much more comfortable than the flea-filled straw in the stable." He gave another deep bow.

Later that evening, after a meal of rice and veg-etables, the monk and Ping sat at a table with their host drinking a dark tea.

"Much has happened to Pei Lei since you passed through here years ago. A warlord by the name of Liu Pen took over the village and all farms in the area. Our Magistrate is corrupt, and Liu Pen bribed him to stay out of this part of the Prefecture. *The Inn of Weary*

Travelers became his headquarters after tossing me, and my staff, out the door."

"I can see the difficulty, Mr. Meng. Have you petitioned the Governor to right this wrong?"

"Yes, Master. I've been told that troops are on the way, and an Imperial Inquisitor will arrive to look into the activities of the corrupt Magistrate. If you stay for another week, you will witness the fight."

"Ping and I will be leaving tomorrow. It sounds like the situation here will be changing."

PING UNDERSTANDS THE LESSON OF CHANGE WITHIN THE DAO

The next day, Master Bao and Ping left Pei Lei and continued their journey. When they stopped for their noon rice, Ping bowed before the monk, his hands clasped in his capacious sleeves.

"Master, please enlighten this ignorant pupil. The first village, Lanchow, had been ravaged by war, but is now a friendly and happy place, with rich fields and content citizens.

"The second village, Pei Lei, was once prosperous and rich, but is now miserable. How does this happen in our great land of the Dragon Throne?"

Master Bao thought for a moment. "The most honored tenet of those of us who follow *The Way* is the acceptance of change. All changes are within the

Flow of the Dao. The forest we traveled through was changing from its summer to autumn beauty, and we accepted that change as the *Will of Heaven*.

"The death of the kindly village elder in Lanchow is part of the cycle of Nature, again, we accept the *Will of Heaven*.

"Changes wrought by the vagaries of humans can be of benefit, as in Lanchow, or destructive, as in Pei Lei.

"The Dragon Throne, as it exists under the *Mandate of Heaven*, will restore harmony to the village of Pei Lei. That is change its citizens will happily accept, and it follows the *Will of Heaven*."

Ping thought long and hard about change. Finally, just as Master Bao was climbing onto his ox, Ping spoke up.

"Because all change is in the *Flow of the Dao*, Master, we therefore accept all change as we accept the sun rising and setting, the seasons passing, and the death of elders."

Master Bao smiled at his pupil. "Yes, Ping. The seasons change, the moon waxes and wanes, dynasties come and go, and people are born and die. A pond empties while another fills, as the endless becoming of yin and yang. All the Universe is in constant transition, yet always in balance and harmony.

"The eternal lesson, Pupil Ping, is that when we

simply observe what's happening from within our inner stillness, and wait upon the *Will of Heaven*, we reflect the equilibrium and balance of the Universe."

Ping's Lesson of Respect

*An attack on Master Bao
is thwarted.*

Master Bao and Ping stopped for the night at a small shelter in the forest. They had traveled from the village of Peng Lui in Qian Zhong to the deep forest of Jiannan Province. After the great ox, Xi, was rubbed, fed, and bedded down for the night, Ping lit a small cooking fire, and the travelers enjoyed their evening rice with vegetables. After he had poured their tea, Student Ping stood, bowed deeply to the monk, his hands clasped inside his capacious sleeves.

"Master, please enlighten this ignorant student. You never douse the fire with water, but sit up watching the embers until they are out. And you will not allow me to dump water on the fire after we are finished cooking our food. All other people we've seen simply pour water on the fire, and then stir the coals to make sure they are out, but you will not do this.

"Please share your reasons for this way of doing things with this humble pupil."

For a long moment, Master Bao sipped his tea, then spoke. "Student Ping. Does the fire not consume wood as food? Does the fire not breath the same air as we, in order to survive? Is not the fire moving while clinging to the wood, much as a human is moving while clinging to the earth?"

"Yes, Master. So, the fire is alive?"

"Perhaps not as a human is alive, but as a fire is alive. Remember, too, all things are in the Universe, and all things are entitled to respect. A friend like this fire is a good example. What did this fire give us this evening, Ping?"

"The fire gave us heat to warm our bodies. It gave us light to see so we didn't trip over roots or stones. It gave us safety, for the wild animals fear fire. It cooked our food, and boiled water for our tea."

"Yes, Ping. It also gave us a hearth, such are found in the kitchens of every home. A fire becomes the spiritual center of a house, and this fire is the spiritual center of our shelter where we will sleep tonight."

"So," Ping said. "The fire is a friend who gives us much."

"Yes, Ping. And if a friend was dying, would you suffocate him so you could sleep sooner? Or would you stay up with your friend until he passed away naturally?"

Ping bowed deeply. "Of course, Master. This obtuse pupil now understands why we treat the fire with such respect. Thank you for this profound lesson."

The next day, Master Bao rode Xi along the trail through the forest. Ping walked alongside. "We will stay at *The Inn of Innocent Slumber* tonight, Ping. It lies a few miles ahead in the town of Han-Yuan. A military post lies just outside the village, so many soldiers will be present."

The travelers arrived in Han-Yuan in the early afternoon. As Master Bao had predicted, many solders strolled throughout the town, some in metal armor and some in Army uniforms of wool.

"We'll rub Xi down and feed him. Giving him proper care is how we show respect for our noble animal."

"Xi is our friend, also," Ping declared.

"Yes, Ping. He is our friend."

After registering at *The Inn of Innocent Slumber*, the travelers took a seat at a table in the restaurant that was part of the inn. The waiter brought them bowls of steaming rice and a large plate of cooked vegetables.

Ping noticed two other tables were occupied by

groups of villagers dressed as craftsmen, and a group of six soldiers, large men in wool uniforms, sat at another table. The soldiers were drinking wine and talking loudly.

Soon, one of the soldiers who had been watching Master Bao and Ping, approached the travelers. He was tall, and had a broad chest, huge arms, and a trimmed ring beard.

"You, Monk," the man announced. "my friends and I have just driven the Mongol Horde from the field, and I alone killed thirty of the enemy. While you sit here and do nothing, we fight and keep the Empire safe. I hate all monks who refuse to fight."

Master Bao stood, and bowed to the man. "We appreciate your sacrifice and duty, Soldier. As you say, we monks do not fight. But we perform other duties for the betterment of the Empire."

Without warning, the soldier swung his open hand at Master Bao's face. But the monk moved his head back quickly and the soldier's slap missed. Another back-handed slap also missed.

The man gave a growled, clenched his teeth, and drew his short sword. He lunged at the monk, but the blade slipped past Master Bao when the monk turned quickly to one side. As the hand holding the sword went past, the monk grasped the man's wrist, and pressed his thumb into the back of the soldier's hand, using a boxer's hold known as "defanging the viper." The sword clattered to the floor.

Still holding the soldier's wrist, Master Bao stepped under the man's outstretched arm, and suddenly bent at the waist. Then, using a boxer's trick called "turning a bull into a bird," he flipped the large man, who flew through the air, landing with a crash on his back. His friends, at first struck silent, burst out with roars of laughter.

"Don't worry, Monk," one of the soldiers said. "We'll take the Sergeant back to the barracks and sober him up. He should have known better than to pick on an old man minding his own business."

The soldiers left while Master Bao and Ping finished eating. As they drank their tea, the manager came up to Master Bao and bowed deeply. "The meal is free, Master Monk. You could have been killed, and the Magistrate would have closed this restaurant. Please accept the meal as my gratitude."

"Thank you for your kindness, Manager. But we'll pay for the meal. Our philosophy requires us to be independent."

Later, as the monk and Ping were standing on the veranda of the restaurant, Ping bowed deeply to Master Bao, his hands clasped inside his capacious sleeves.

"Please enlighten this ignorant student, Master.

You taught me respect for the fire and in all things in the Universe.

"Lack of respect caused the man to attack you, and disturb the peace of the restaurant, yet he was filled with wine and anger. Like the lightening bolt that causes a forest fire, his anger was beyond his control. What then is the duty of a monk?"

Master Bao thought for a long moment before answering. "A forest fire, with its massive damage and hardship, can be caused by a lightening bolt, truly the *Will of Heaven*. The people respond by building fire lanes and breaks, to keep the fire from spreading to the village. The difficulty is not ignored because it due to fate or chance.

"A man filled with wine and anger can cause damage and hardship, but he also is subject to the *Will of Heaven*.

"Just as we keep the forest fire from destroying the village, so we keep the angry and drunk man from doing damage and creating hardship. His humiliation followed his choice to attack an old man.

"As a *Follower of the Way*, my duty today was to prevent damage and hardship. Nothing more."

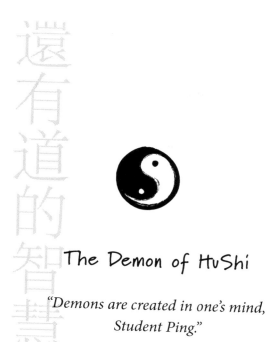

The Demon of HuShi

"Demons are created in one's mind,
Student Ping."

Master Bao rode his great ox, Xi, along a well-traveled road through Hedong Providence in the northern part of the Empire. His pupil, Ping, walked alongside.

Ping glanced up and saw a few white fluffy clouds floating serenely in an azure sky. Both sides of the road were flanked by waving tall green and yellow grasses.

"This is a most pleasant road, and a pleasant day," Ping remarked. "It is neither too hot nor too cool."

"Yes, Ping. And we can enjoy the present moment to its fullest. In a short time, we'll be in the village of HuShi. I've never been in this is part of the providence before, but I'm confident we'll be well-received."

An hour later, just outside HuShi, a sweating man dressed as a laborer came running toward them pulling a two-wheel cart on which sat a woman holding a small girl. Two young boys ran behind the cart.

"Master," the man shouted when he spotted Master Bao and Ping. "Run back from where you came. The Demon of HuShi will rip you limb from limb, and devour the boy."

Ping watched as the family rushed past, then looked at Master Bao sitting quietly on Xi.

"I don't think I would like to be devoured by a demon, Master." He folded his hands inside his capacious sleeves and bowed deeply to the monk. "Perhaps we should seek a different village for our evening rice."

Master Bao dismounted and smiled as he adjusted Xi's saddle blanket. "Demons are created in one's mind, Student Ping. They spring from pain and anger, carried deep inside. Often, when fed by wine and frustration, they manifest in a physical form that can cause great destruction."

Ping bowed again. "Can they tear a man limb from limb, as the villager said? Or devour a student? Can the *Dao* protect a monk and his pupil from such a great evil?"

"The *Mighty Dao*, Ping, does not recognize good or evil. Like the mountain stream, it nourishes all who thirst. Good and Evil are known only to humans.

"But it does recognize harmony and disharmony, balance and unbalance. To fight a demon means bringing harmony and balance to one who has twisted away from the *Flow of the Dao*."

The monk climbed aboard Xi. "Come, Ping. You may rest your worries. Hideous demons live only in the minds of the fearful. Let us see this demon for ourselves. Perhaps we can help someone in need."

As they entered HuShi, the travelers were nearly run down by mobs of people fleeing the wrath of the demon. Master Bao stopped one man dressed as a craftsman. "Kind Sir," he asked, "Where can I find this demon who you flee?"

"He lives on this very street," the man replied. "Run away, for he will smell the warm blood of you and your young companion and find you quickly enough. He killed the potter, Chou Hue, and now lives in his hut. Flee with us while you still have a chance."

"Have you seen this demon?" Master Bao asked. "What does he look like?"

"I've never seen him myself, but it is said he is ten feet tall, green in color with the horns of a ram. His eyes glow orange, I'm told. But I mustn't linger or I'll be his next meal."

Further on, Master Bao and Ping were surrounded by men, women, and children carrying their meager possessions in bundles as they fled down the street.

The monk stopped a woman who was pushing a young child in a cart. "Good woman," he asked. "where can I find this demon who you flee?"

"He lives further up this very street," the woman said. "Run away, for he will smell the warm blood of you and your young companion and find you quickly enough. He slayed the potter, Chou Hue, and took over his hut. Flee with us while you still have a chance."

"Have you seen this demon?" Master Bao asked. "What does he look like?"

"I've never seen him myself, but it is said he is short and round, bright red in color, with great sharp teeth and long claws. His eyes are yellow, I'm told. But I mustn't linger or I'll be his next meal."

Finally, the travelers came to the end of the street where sat a small stone hut on a piece of unattended land. The front yard was covered in dry plants and stones. Ping stood behind the ox, as Master Bao strode up to the wooden door. The monk knocked loudly.

A loud roar, like an angry tiger, came from within, and purple smoke, smelling of spoiled eggs, poured from under the door. Ping stepped further back, covering his mouth with his sleeves, but kept his eyes fastened on his Master.

When the echo of the roar died away, Master Bao knocked again. This time, a scream like an injured gibbon came from within, and green smoke, smelling of decomposed meat, poured from under the door. Ping coughed into his sleeves, but kept his eyes fastened on his Master.

When the echo of the scream died away, Master Bao knocked again. This time, the door was abruptly pulled open to reveal a skinny man, his gray hair and beard in violent disarray. His eyes were runny, his face covered in boils, and his mouth drawn into a fierce snarl. "What do you want, you fool? Can't you see I'm a sick man? You've just been exposed to the plague."

"Perhaps I can help, Chou Hue" Master Bao said. "By your appearance alone, I can see that you have a disease that resembles the plague. But it can be cured. Your boils are not from a disease, but from the bite of a small insect that lives in sleeping clothes and lays eggs in unkempt beards and hair."

"What? I've been burning horrible smelling plants and animals in my fireplace to keep the villagers away. The cries of my pet tiger and pet gibbon have helped. Now, you tell me I don't have the plague, but bites from some insect?"

"Yes. You must burn your mattress and bedding. If you stop trying to keep the villagers away, they will help you find new, clean bedding. And you must trim your beard and hair."

"I will do as you say, Master, for you are a wise monk."

Master Bao handed the potter a small jar filled with a white cream. "After you wash in warm water and soap, put this ointment on your boils. If you follow my directions, you will be free of your troubles in three days."

Potter Chou Hue broke down in sobs. "I love the people of this village so much that I feared spreading the plague among them. I pulled the tail of my pet tiger to make him roar, and twisted the ear of my pet gibbon to make him scream. The smoke did the rest."

The next day, Master Bao and Ping left the village, taking the road to the next town. When they stopped to eat their noon rice, Ping bowed to the monk, his hands folded inside his capacious sleeves.

"Please, Master. Enlighten this ignorant pupil. How did you know the evil demon of HuShi was just an ill old man? All the villagers were filled with panic. The tales they told were of a fearsome, powerful demon. Yet, you showed no concern."

Master Bao sat on a mat in the shade of a tree with wide leaves. "Please sit, student Ping, and I will tell you about demons, then we will have our noon rice."

After Ping had spread his mat and sat, the monk took a deep breath.

"Demons are people who are in pain, Ping, and their pain is caught in a loop. The pain can be a wound, or grief, or rejection from others. The most fearsome demons are when a powerful emotion, such as love, is lost for any reason. The pain feels like a fire inside that is unable to be quenched by water or wine. This leads to disharmony in the very core of their being, and blockages to their yin and yang energies overwhelms their mind and body.

"The imbalance in the person's yin and yang soon leads to strange behavior, often harmful to both friends and strangers. Others become fearful because they don't understand and begin to make up desperate stories in their minds. When something is unknown, it is in the nature of humans to invent reasons and stories to explain the event.

"In the case of the potter Chou Hue, his disease clashed with his love for the villagers, causing great pain and imbalance. While he believed he needed to keep the villagers away from him for their own safety, he missed them terribly and, in spite of his deliberate actions, felt rejected and alone. The townspeople reacted to his actions with fear."

Ping nodded. "This fear then caused the demon/person more pain, and the loop was completed," he said. "But Master, you knew none of this when we spoke to the villagers. They described a monster of wicked proportions who devoured human beings."

Master Bao chuckled. "As I said, demons crawl out of an abyss of pain, which can sometimes be cured.

As *Followers of the Way*, it is our mission to heal those in pain and suffering when we are able. Fear in the villagers was a result of misunderstanding of the *Flow of the Dao*, which does not recognize evil and good, or life and death.

"Besides, Ping, I knew we had nothing to fear. You and I are much too stringy and tough for a demon to devour. They prefer softer monks and students."

The Joy of the Present

*"This moment is all we have
in which to live our joy."*

Master Bao rode his ox, Xi, along a trail that led through a beautiful forest of vibrant green leaves, and ground cover of blooming flowers. His pupil, Ping, walked alongside his master.

"This is a most beautiful forest," Ping said. "And the day is sunny, with no clouds in the sky."

Master Bao turned to Ping and smiled. "How do you feel, Ping, on such a day in such a forest?"

"My heart is overflowing, Master, with peace and joy. My feet and my pack are light, and the road is smooth and level."

Master Bao nodded, "Feel the breeze, Student Ping, the warmth of the sun. Smell the fragrant flowers.

What do you taste, hear? Welcome those sensations, and keep them as a part of you. This is the joy of the present."

Just ahead, near two farmhouses, two men were standing a few feet apart shouting at each other. They were dressed in the long shirt and wide trousers of farmers. Two women, their heads bowed and their hands folded in front of them, stood together to one side.

Master Bao stopped Xi and sat watching the men, while Ping stood behind the great ox.

When the men noticed the monk and his pupil, they stopped yelling, turned toward the travelers, and bowed.

"You are having a loud disagreement," Master Bao said. "Can we be of some assistance."

"I am called Wang," the man on the right said, bowing deeply, "and I am the owner of this farm and this herd of sheep." He pointed to the farmhouse behind him. "This kind woman is my wife." The woman closest to him bowed.

"And I am called Liu," the man on the left said, with a deep bow, "and I am the owner of this farm and this herd of goats." He pointed to the farmhouse behind him. "This gracious woman is my wife." The woman closest to him bowed.

"What seems to be the trouble?" the monk asked.

Wang spoke first. "This miserable dog's breath is a sheep thief, and now his unfortunate son wants to marry my beautiful daughter. I won't permit a thief's blood to dishonor my blameless family."

Liu shouted, his face red, "I have never stolen anything in my life, but I know you are a goat thief, dung beetle that you are."

Master Bao looked at the two men. "When was the sheep stolen?" he asked.

Wang answered, "It was his great-grandfather who, in the dead of night, crept into my great-grandfather's sheep pen and sneaked off with a ewe."

"And it was your great-grandfather, "Liu replied loudly, "who snuck into my great-grandfather's goat pen and stole a buck."

The two women sighed deeply at the same time, and the wife of Wang said, "Master, this has been going on since the summer of the flood (75 years), and the families have been fighting ever since."

The wife of Liu stepped forward. "Now, our children who love each other and wish to marry, find these two foolish old men standing in their way."

Together, the women exclaimed, "Can you help solve our problem, Master?"

Master Bao thought for a long moment.

"Mr. Wang and Mr. Liu, you are living the wrong story. You are living a story that is many seasons in the past, rather than living in this time. The past is a closed door, unchangeable. Both of you have been carrying the poison of these events long past, and now it seems to be spilling into the lives of your young children, robbing them of their joy of the present."

Both Wang and Liu looked ashamed and hung their heads.

"Here is what I suggest," Master Bao continued. "Mr. Wang, give Mr. Liu one of your sheep. And you, Mr. Liu, give Mr. Wang one of your goats. In time, you may exchange more animals and build a flock of sheep and a herd of goats. By living your story in the present, both can prosper."

"I agree," said Mr. Wang. "I will give a ewe to Mr. Liu. In the sheep breeding season, he can have one of my rams visit the ewe."

"I also agree," said Mr. Liu. "I will give a nanny goat to Mr. Wang. In the goat breeding season, he can have one of my bucks visit the nanny."

That night, the Master and his pupil stayed at *The Inn of Pilgrim's Rest* in the small village of Han. The next day, they resumed their travels onto the endless grassland of Han-Lu.

Later that morning, as the two travelers moved out onto the vast plain, the monk noticed that Ping, watching the clouds gathering in the sky, shifted his small pack from one shoulder to the other.

"How do you feel, Ping, on such a day in this grassy plain?"

"My heart is overflowing with apprehension, Master. My feet and my pack feel heavy, and the road is rocky."

With a nod, Master Bao turned to Ping. "Feel the breeze, Student Ping, and the warmth of the sun. Smell the fragrance of the grasslands. What do you taste, hear? Welcome those sensations into you, and keep them as part of you. This is the joy of the present."

Master Bao dismounted from Xi and stood looking out over the grassland. "Yesterday is past, Ping, and you have deep memories of a beautiful forest, colorful flowers, and a smooth road. Tomorrow, the road may be smooth or rocky, the sky filled with sun or rain.

"Yesterday and tomorrow are mere wisps of mist, Student Ping. We cannot change yesterday, for it is past. And we don't know what the road ahead will be, for the future is not known to us mortals.

"This moment is all we have in which to live our joy.

"The future may be filled with either fear or pleasure, unknown to us now.

"This present is what we have. The beauty of the grassland, the scent of the earth, the humming of the bees, and the color of the flowers. Live with what is here now, and not what was or what will be, and you will know true joy."

"Come, Ping, the clouds are gathering and it will soon rain. The future is hidden, but I know what the clouds mean when they darken, for I learned that from my past. I also learned the next inn is only a short distance from here."

Master Bao climbed on his ox. "We learn from the past, Ping, so we can plan for the future. But we gather joy from the present."

That evening, the travelers were warm and dry in *The Inn of Happy Repose*, as the sky opened, and the sound of the rain, beating on the roof, filled Master Bao and Ping with joy.

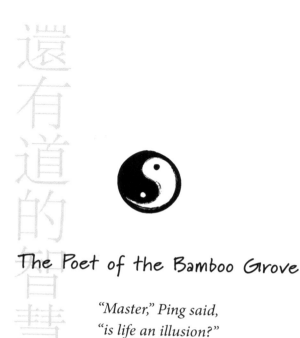

The Poet of the Bamboo Grove

"Master," Ping said,
"is life an illusion?"

Master Bao rode his great ox, Xi, along a trail in the southern province of Lingnan. His student Ping walked alongside.

"This part of Lingnan is thought to be haunted by ghosts, Master," Ping said. He kept sweeping his gaze of the deep forest quickly from one side of the road to the other.

Master Bao asked, "Do you not fear your head will become loose if you keep twisting it back and forth?"

"Master, I keep seeing strange creatures moving among the trees. And it is well known that Weretigers roam this very forest. Is that not true, Master?"

"It is true that I have heard those stories," Master Bao responded. After a brief moment, he continued. "Tonight, we will stay in the village of Hong Wa, a few miles distant from here. There is an inn in Hong Wa known for its tasty vegetable dishes, cooked with secret, complex mixtures of spices."

Ping's face broke into a wide smile. "I'm happy we'll not need to spend the night in this forest, Master."

Just ahead, a man, dressed in a patched and ragged blue robe, sat by the side of the road playing a happy melody on a reed flute. He was completely bald and beardless. Next to him on the ground was a beautiful lute with six strings.

When they reached the man, Master Bao stopped Xi and dismounted. The man stopped playing, stood, and bowed to the travelers. "Greetings, Monk," the man said. "For where are you bound?"

"Hong Wa," responded Master Bao, returning the bow.

"Ah. A noisy village filled with hard-working people."

"So I've heard. Are you from Hong Wa?"

"No, I am Liu Hing, and I spend my days on the road or in this forest. I'm waiting for some friends who I meet each afternoon. Nearby is our special place where we play music, sing, and drink wine. We are "The Poets of the Bamboo Grove." It's a merry time, and you and the boy are welcome to join us."

"Thank you for the kind invitation, but we must travel on to Hong Wa."

The man shook his head. "A noisy place, Monk, filled with people who toil and suffer, day after day. They don't understand life is an illusion without meaning. Work and then die, all without meaning. And this forest is filled with their dancing ghosts."

An hour after leaving Liu Hing, who had resumed his place sitting beside the road now playing his lute, Master Bao and Ping stopped in a small shady field near the road. Ping laid out a mat and prepared the noonday rice for Master Bao and himself. After eating, Ping stood before the monk and bowed deeply, his hands clasped in his capacious sleeves.

"Master, please enlighten this ignorant student. What did Liu Hing mean about the forest filled with ghosts? I'm fearful of ghosts."

"Please sit down on the mat, Student Ping. Pour yourself another cup of tea."

After Ping sat with a cup of tea, Master Bao began.

"When we are born, a Spirit comes from heaven and enters the body of the baby. The body is heavy, and belongs to the Earth. When it comes time to die, its Spirit, which is light, rises back up to heaven, and the heavy body remains on Earth, where it becomes part of the Earth itself.

"As you know, the word for ghost is also the word for 'return,' and a ghost is simply a Spirit who is returning to heaven. It is on a journey, dancing as it leaves its body, and is nothing to be feared."

"Thank you, Master. Now that I understand ghosts are dancing spirits on a journey to heaven, they hold no terror for me."

"This is a quiet shady field, Ping, and you've brewed a fine cup of tea. Do you have any other questions before we resume our journey?"

"Yes, Master. What did Liu Hing mean when he said life is an illusion?"

"Liu Hing is quite famous among philosophers. He and his Poets of the Bamboo Grove, believe life is a short journey, like the breath of an ox in winter, and the flash of a lightning bolt.

"So as our lives, being so far from permanent, show perhaps that nothing is permanent. And, since no one will remember us in a hundred years, why worry about social conventions and approval of others now?

"To them, life on earth, with all our rules and laws, is merely an illusion we have agreed to follow."

Ping brightened up. "It reminds me of the story you told me long ago about the august Zhuangzi. He said he can't know for certain if he is Zhuangzi dreaming he is a butterfly, or a butterfly asleep dreaming he is

Zhuangzi. So then all life may be an illusion, a dream.

"I will think deeply on this, Master, for it is confusing."

Hours later, as the travelers journeyed up the main street of Hong Wa, Ping asked the monk,

"Master, is life an illusion?"

"Perhaps, Ping. However, while the hunger in my belly may also be an illusion, the scent of spices coming from the kitchen of this inn seems quite real. Why don't we decide whether life is an illusion after we try the vegetables? Philosophy should never be discussed on an empty stomach."

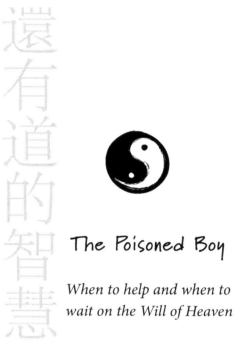

The Poisoned Boy

When to help and when to
wait on the Will of Heaven

Master Bao rode his great ox, Xi, along a road that ran through a burned over forest. His pupil, Ping, walked alongside.

"This providence of Jiannan has suffered a long drought, Ping. The trees became dry and a fire last year burned this large area. Many people and animals perished in the blaze."

Ping sniffed, smelling charred wood. "Many trees and plants died, also."

The monk smiled at his pupil's awareness of all life, and the universality of suffering.

Soon, the travelers reached the village of Pooyang, spared from the fire by the river Que that ran between the town and the forest. "Ahead is *The Inn of Forever Light*, Ping. We'll see if they have a room available."

Before they reached the inn, however, they became aware of a group of villagers gathered at the door of a hovel, speaking quietly among themselves.

"There is a monk," one of the men on the edge of the crowd shouted. "Perhaps he can save little Meng Kee."

Master Bao dismounted. "What is the trouble?"

Just then the door flew open and a woman, crying uncontrollably, rushed out. "Oh, Master Monk. You must save my son," she said, sobbing. "He is dying. He ate poison berries from a plant along the river."

The woman tugged Master Bao's sleeve, pulling him into her hovel. After handing the reins of Xi to one of the villagers, Ping followed. A man with a short beard, dressed in the leather apron of a craftsman, sat on a mat next to a fireplace where a single-log fire burned. He held a small boy on his lap who appeared to be sleeping. Tears, glistening in the firelight, ran down the man's face.

The monk examined the boy and saw purple spots covering his face and chest. He noted that the boy was breathing shallowly, his limbs slack.

"Place the child on his back on the table, Crafts-man," Master Bao said. "Ping, go to the well and get a fresh pot of water, and get my pouch from Xi. Then, this kind woman will boil the water."

When the child was lying on the table, Master Bao, starting at the his head, made a motion with two fingers as if chopping the air above the boy. He then worked his way down the child's body, finishing just after Ping returned. Then, the monk moved his open hands back and forth above the boy.

"Ping, watch closely to what I am doing. The poison blocked his *Qi* channels, so I first broke up the blocks. Now I'm pouring *Qi* into him."

"Are you using your own *Qi*, Master?"

"I am but a tube, like a bamboo shoot. The *Qi* is from the Universe, running through me. I'm merely directing its power."

Within minutes, the boy's spots began to disappear. Then, he opened his eyes. His mother and father, crying out with joy, attracted the villagers who poured into the house and surrounded the family.

"Here are some tea leaves, my good woman," the monk said. He took a small package from his pouch. "Let your son rest, but give him a cup of tea twice today. That will complete his healing."

The mother and father dropped to their knees and knocked their foreheads on the floor three times, wailing their gratitude, tears streaming down their faces. "Our little Kee is all we have, and we thought we had lost him."

The rest of the villagers also kneeled in front of the monk.

"There is no need to kneel," Master Bao said, "I'm just a poor monk, not an official of the Dragon Throne."

After they left the home, the travelers walked to the inn, leading Xi. "There is a stable behind the inn, Ping. We'll get Xi settled down, then register at the inn.

"It will then be time for our evening rice, and my nose tells me this inn has a fine restaurant."

While they were rubbing down Xi, Ping said, with a deep bow, "Life and death are both in the *Flow of the Dao*, Master. Yet, you saved the life of that sick child. How do we know when to act and when to await on the *Will of Heaven*?"

"Ah, Ping. As *Followers of the Way*, we must do our best to relieve pain. We must be kind, caring and, when able, bring our knowledge of healing to those who suffer. The *Dao*, being the flow of all nature and therefore life, demands we help.

"Tomorrow, we will check on the boy, Student Ping, but right now, the scent of spiced rice calls to us."

The Third Princess

"Who is this monk who does not bow to the Dragon Throne?"

Master Bao rode his great ox, Xi, along a road paved with flat stones. His pupil, Ping, strode alongside.

"The 'Summer Palace' is in this province, Ping. If the Emperor and his family are in residence, we will be stopped by Imperial Guards before we reach the village of Hwe-Shin."

"Perhaps we'll get a glimpse of some of the people from the royal court," Ping said.

"Perhaps," the monk responded.

After about an hour, the travelers stopped at a well near the side of the rode. The well-tender bowed to Master Bao and handed him a cup of water. The monk waited until Xi and Ping had drunk before accepting the offered container.

"You come at an auspicious time, Master," the well-tender said, as the three men sat on a bench under a ginkgo tree. "The Third Princess is in residence at the Summer Palace. As you probably know, the Third Princess is the kindest member of the Dragon Throne, and a great scholar."

Master Bao sipped his water. "Yes, I have heard she speaks many dialects, and meets daily with learned men."

"True, Master. My sister knows one of the cooks in the palace and I hear much about the Third Princess. She surrounds herself with men who know the ways of Nature, and the wisest counselors in the Empire. Also, her calligraphy is renowned and her poetry is said to be the finest in the land."

"She sounds like a young woman of many accomplishments. Thank you for the water, but now we must travel to Hwe-Shin by nightfall. Come, Ping."

About an hour later, they heard a loud furor coming from the direction of Hwe-Shin. Cymbals clashing and drums pounding heralded the approach of a group of music makers. As they passed by, they were followed by fifty mounted lancers, the sun reflecting off their shiny bronze armor and the points of their spears. Coming behind the horsemen was an ornate closed palanquin, trimmed in gold and silver, carried by eight men. A second palanquin, not nearly as ornate, was close behind. Three luggage carts pulled by oxen, followed the second conveyance, and a large group of colorfully garbed men and women walked behind the carts. They, in turn, were followed by fifty swordsmen, their iron boots clanking on the flat paving stones.

"It's the Third Princess," Ping shouted. He jumped to the side of the rode, dropped to his knees, and placed his forehead on the ground.

Master Bao dismounted and stood beside his ox. "I believe you are right, Ping. It surely must be royalty, for no one else would make such a commotion."

As the ornate palanquin began to pass Master Bao, a young woman's voice cried out, "Stop!" The entire parade came to a halt.

Immediately, the foot soldiers ran to surround the palanquin, swords drawn. A veiled face appeared at the window.

"Who is this monk who does not bow to the Dragon Throne?" questioned the Third Princess.

From the second litter, a heavy-jowled man, dressed in elaborate robes, jumped out and ran to stand outside the lady's window, his hands clasped inside his sleeves.

"It is a monk of the *Daoist* philosophy, Your Highness," the man explained. "They are rascals who bow to no one. I believe this one is called Master Bao."

For several seconds, silence reigned. "Come here, Monk. Let me look at you," the young lady said.

The soldiers parted, leaving a path to the window of the palanquin. Master Bao stepped up to the window, past the ranks of swordsmen. A large man wearing the armor and insignia of an Army Captain stood next to the palanquin, his face twisted into a scowl. His hand was on the pommel of his broadsword.

"Why do you not bow, Monk?" the Third Princess asked. "I could have you beheaded right here in the road."

"And I could lose my head right here in the road. What would that avail of either of us?"

There was a pause of several seconds. "You are arrogant, Monk."

"No, my Princess. I am honest. Honesty is often mistaken for arrogance."

Another pause. "Do you not fear death, Monk?"

Master Bao smiled. "Life and death are the same in the *Dao*. Like the grass, death comes in winter, and, in spring, life follows death. Merely a change in form according to the season."

After another long pause, the Third Princess raised her voice. "Minister Choi," she said, "have the Royal Tent prepared. I will have lunch with this monk and the child with his face in the dirt." She looked at Master Bao again. "I'm sure sharing my rice will not offend your philosophical sensibilities. Bring the boy."

The Minister threw his hands into the air, gave a deep sigh, and began to bellow orders. There was a mad scramble while servants unloaded one of the luggage carts. Master Bao took Ping's arm and drew him to his feet. The two watched perhaps fifty men and women quickly erect a large, colorful round tent in a nearby field, fill it with carpets and cushions, then load a table under the canopy with wooden bowls of color-ful fruit and vegetables. Two servers brought ornate rice jars and vases filled with a variety of flowers.

"Bring the second chair for the monk," the Third Princess told a soldier, as she eased herself into an ornate cathedra.

"Princess," Minister Choi said with a deep bow to the lady, "the second chair is for distinguished guests of noble birth. It is not for peasants."

"This man has a noble look about him, Choi. Do as you're told or you'll walk back to the palace carrying your head in a bag."

When the young woman removed her veils, Ping stood wide-eyed, gazing at her beauty. Master Bao reached a finger under Ping's chin and closed the boy's mouth.

The rice from the clay pots was warm, and had a

mild, spice flavor. The Third Princess, after her taster sampled the dishes, barely touched her food. Master Bao and Ping each consumed a bowl of rice, and a helping of fruit and vegetables.

The meal was eaten in silence, but the table was hardly cleared when the Third Princess addressed Master Bao.

"I am not as ignorant of your *Daoism* as you may think, Master Bao. We have many learned scholars in the royal court who are familiar with all forms of religion and philosophy. For example, I know of your ideas of *Yin* and *Yang*."

Master Bao nodded politely. "Your knowledge and wisdom are well known, Your Highness."

"Yes. People do talk. If my scholars are not mistaken, *Yin* is part of *Yang*, and *Yang* is contained in *Yin*, the two always becoming the other. How is this, Monk? Can love, for example, ever be part of hate?"

"*Yin* and *Yang* are complementary forces, my Princess. They only appear to be opposites, but are always in balance with one another. Reality is a harmony of things that, to our human nature, only seem opposite.

"Love," Master Bao continued, "has indifference as its complementary opposite, not hate. And, as we well know, love is always in danger of becoming indifference."

The Third Princess smiled. "Well said, Master Bao. But what then of hate? My Captain, here," she motioned to the man standing behind her chair, "despises any man who comes close to me. What is hate's 'complementary opposite?'"

"Hate is a strong *Yang* emotion leading to disharmony. It's *Yin* complement would be harmony of spirit and mind."

"Do you hear that, Captain? Your hate leads to disharmony, but I like you this way, You protect me from evil." The Third Princess paused while a handmaiden poured tea into delicate bone china cups. "What does your philosophy say of good and evil, Master Bao? In the royal court, there is much evil, constant plotting and fighting."

"Good and evil are not part of the flow of Nature, and therefore not part of the *Flow of the Dao*. For the follower of the *Daoist Way*, there is no absolute moral right and wrong.

"However, there are consequences for one's actions. The fox is not evil for eating the farmers' chickens. It's his nature to hunt and kill. But to the farmer, the loss of his chickens to the fox is evil, and he will hunt and kill the fox. So, although not evil, the fox will suffer for his actions, which the farmer will view as evil."

Minister Choi entered the tent and whispered into the Third Princess' ear. As she stood and reattached her veils, Master Bao and Ping came to their feet.

"A most enlightening talk, Master Bao. I would like you to come to the palace and become part of my retinue. We could converse far into the night, and your wisdom would be of great value to the Dragon Throne. Would you agree to do that?"

"Ah, Princess," Master Bao said. "I'm honored by your request, but I can help both the Dragon Throne and the people of this Empire if I remain a humble, itinerant monk, with my student, Ping."

The Third Princess nodded and bowed deeply to Master Bao.

Both he and Ping returned the bow.

Later, after the Third Princess and her entourage had moved on, Ping approached Master Bao and gave a deep bow. "Master. The Third Princess offered you a comfortable and prosperous position in the Palace. In time, because of your wisdom and knowledge, you would have great influence in the handling of important affairs of state. Yet you turned her down. Please enlighten this ignorant pupil and explain why you did not accept her kind offer?"

Master Bao smiled. "What are some of the principles of *Followers of the Way*, Student Ping?"

"Acceptance of life as we find it," Ping replied. "Reverence for Nature, and seek Harmony in Nature."

"And what of our personal characteristics, Ping?"

"No status, no competition, no self-righteousness. And we value Harmony and Equanimity above all else." Ping bowed while reciting the tenets of *The Way*.

"A court a not a place of no status, no competition, no self-righteousness. As a humble, itinerant monk, I can follow *The Way* unencumbered by the mere trappings of power and wealth.

"Real power and wealth resides, not in the halls of the Dragon Throne, Student Ping, but in the harmony of the *Silence Within*."

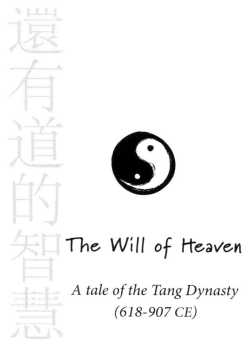

The Will of Heaven

A tale of the Tang Dynasty
(618-907 CE)

Master Bao rode his great ox, Xi, along a trail that ran between two villages in the province of Hedong in the northern region of the Empire. His student, Ping, walked alongside.

"Master," Ping said, "we were fortunate to find shelter in the village of Lanhi when the storm broke yesterday. If we had been on the road, we would have been soaked and cold. Because of our good luck, we were warm, dry, and well fed."

"Yes," the monk replied. "Luck was with us yesterday."

In the road ahead, two men were walking toward Master Bao and Ping. One of the men was dressed in fine robes of silk, while the other had a patched shirt and trousers. The first man had slippers of gold, while the second man was barefoot.

As the men approached, Ping noticed they were of the same height, age, and same beard length, but while one's beard was neatly trimmed, the other's was scraggly.

Both men stepped to the side of the road and bowed deeply to Master Bao. The monk stopped Xi, dismounted, and returned the bow, as did Ping.

"Greetings, Master," the first man said."It is an auspicious happenstance that we should meet a wise monk just at this moment. We have a problem we would like to present to you for enlightenment. Please hear us out."

"Of course," Master Bao replied. "I would be honored to offer whatever aid I can."

"My name is Liu Fang," the man dressed in silk said. "This is my twin brother, Liu Mo. Our problem is one of luck, and has been vexing us for the past two years."

"As my brother said," the man dressed in the cloth shirt and trousers said. "My name is Liu Mo, and my luck has been horrible. My brother has had wonderful luck, and we don't understand why our destinies are so different."

Master Bao looked from one to the other. Both

were handsome young men, and both had spoken clearly. Neither seemed angry or melancholy. But one obviously had prospered while the other hadn't. "Please tell me more," he said.

"Our father was a successful cabinetmaker," Liu Fang said. "His work was renowned throughout the Empire, and many of his carved cabinets are in the richest homes. When he died, he left his tools and plans to both Liu Mo and me. We had trained with him since we were old enough to hold a mallet, and both of us had learned all of his secrets."

Liu Mo continued the tale. "We decided to split up the unfinished work of our father, each taking the same number and type. All were of the highest quality, and we knew we could finish them as beautifully as our father had.'

"So I moved to the Guannei Province so we wouldn't be competing with each other," Liu Fang said.

"And that's where my bad luck came in," Liu Mo said. "While Liu Fang sells his cabinets to the rich, I'm doomed to failure. A fire caused by a careless assistant burned my entire warehouse full of not only my work, but the unfinished cabinets of my father. Until I can show my work to people, and they can see how beautiful my work is, I cannot put food on my table. All my tools were destroyed in the fire."

Liu Fang shook his head. "The unfinished cabinets my father left me have sold for several gold bars, and now my woodworking is selling faster than I can produce it. When I returned just today, after two years, I saw the pitiable state Liu Mo is in."

Master Bao smiled. "You seem to get along well. Why don't you work together to build up Liu Mo's business? Meanwhile, while you have much and your brother has little, why not loan him enough to feed him until you both are successful?"

"Oh, I have, Master," Liu Fang said. "We have started a business together and I will put both of our names on the sign over the door to our workshop. And I have given him two gold bars to feed and cloth him. We were on our way to the clothier in the next town now."

"Then what is the problem you wish me to address?"

"Liu Mo and I are alike in most respects," Liu Fang said. "Why did fortune smile on me and not on Liu Mo? How can one twin have such good luck and the other suffer?"

The monk smiled. "When we cannot find a reason for something happening, we call it an accident," Master Bao began. "Accidents in Nature are called 'Chance,' but when accidents happen to people, we call it 'Luck.'

"Chance, luck, fate, destiny, coincidence, accident.

"All happenings within the *Dao* are workings of the *Will of Heaven*, and the ancient sages tell us that the *Will of Heaven* is often beyond our understanding. Sometimes happenings bring us prosperity, and sometimes poverty. It is not for us to always know the reason."

Much later, Master Bao and Ping shared their evening rice at a wayside restaurant. After eating, Ping stood and bowed deeply to the monk. "Master, please enlighten this ignorant student. Why is one twin so unfortunate to have his warehouse burn, while the other is prosperous? Why does heaven choose one to live in poverty?"

"There is a story told by the august Monk Ma Po that may help you understand. Two farmers had adjoining land. On one farmer's fields, the soft rain fell, the soil was fertile, and the crops grew in abundance. On the other farm, the sun baked the soil, the rain didn't fall. The crops were stunted and dry.

"Finally, the farmer with the rich crops went to the poor farmer and told him they should switch farms for one year to see if the rains were due to the *Will of Heaven* or due to the diligence and good character of the successful farmer himself.

"It made no difference. Good character and diligence were not rewarded with soft rains. The crops on the poor farm remained stunted and dry. The two men became good friends and helped each other at harvest time.

"What is the lesson here, Student Ping?"

"This poor student still fails to understand the reason for the difference in the rainfall of the two farms."

Master Bao was silent for a long moment before he spoke. "In the story, the two farmers became friends because of the difficulties of one and the generosity of the other. Would this have happened if not for the difference in rainfall? Would the twin brother cabinetmakers have gone into business together without the burning of the warehouse?

"As *Followers of the Way*, we accept that Heaven has a plan we cannot see or understand. Fortune or misfortune are the providence of the *Will of Heaven* and for us mortals, the plan remains a mystery. We do our part by being kind, gentle, and following the *Flow of the Dao*."

The Vanishing Gold

*"Independence, equanimity, and kindness,
are the goals of the Followers of the Way."*

Master Bao rode his water buffalo, Xi, along a well-traveled road in Lingnan Province. His pupil, Ping, walked alongside.

"The weather is becoming warm, Student Ping, and we can rest in the shade just ahead. There is a well-known spring in a dove tree glade where we can get fresh water."

Ping nodded in acknowledgment.

A short time later, the travelers arrived at the spring, unsaddled Xi, and led the ox to a watering trough. After seeing that the animal was well-cared for, Master Bao sat on a bench provided for weary pilgrims. Student Ping drank deeply from the bubbling spring, then filled their water bags.

A man, dressed as a merchant, sat in a secluded area of the glade, his head sunk forward, as if deep in thought. A well-bred unsaddled horse stood nearby, its bridle tied to a tree branch.

The man then looked up, stood, and walked toward the monk and Ping. Master Bao noticed the merchant had wide shoulders, a broad chest, and a strong stride. He also noticed the hilt of a sword under the merchant's robe.

Master Bao rose as the man approached. The merchant clasped his left fist into his right palm, and bowed deeply to the monk. "Forgive this intrusion, Master Monk, but I find it auspicious that we meet at this difficult time."

The monk returned the bow. "How can a humble monk aid the famous Prefect Wang Chu?"

"You recognize me. Master Monk." He sighed deeply. "But not a Prefect for long. The Imperial Censor Ch'ang Hao is on his way."

"You must begin at the start of your troubles, Prefect Wang, for my pupil and I have not heard of your difficulty. When I last saw you, you were a Magistrate and well on your way to becoming a Governor, or an Imperial Court Judge, such was your reputation for honesty and integrity."

"Whom am I addressing, Monk?"

"I am called Bao, and this is my pupil, Ping."

"Then this truly is an auspicious meeting, for I have heard you are a wise monk, and I have need of your wisdom. My difficulties fall in the mysterious spiritual realm, as much as the physical. Perhaps we need a *Daoist* idea on my case, rather than a Confucian lawbook."

The men sat on the bench while Ping stood nearby and listened closely to their conversation.

"As you say, Master Bao, I was a successful Magistrate for ten years, with a reputation for integrity. I accepted no bribes and punished court personal who stooped to dishonesty. I was appointed Prefect as a reward for my honesty, with ten districts under me. And then last week, disaster struck."

Prefect Wang took a small drink of water from a gourd before continuing.

"Li Chia is one of the richest men in Chang-Sha district, and a local tyrant. After receiving information from other merchants that he was smuggling silk and grain from across the border to avoid paying taxes, I started an investigation. First, he tried to bribe me. Then I discovered he was trying to bribe my chief clerk.

I decided it was time to bring him to court, even though the investigation was barely started. That's when the real trouble began.

"A merchant brought a chest of gold bars to the

Prefecture for safe keeping. It's not unusual for the Prefect to store large quantities of gold or silver in our locked room. It is guarded night and day, and no one, other than the Prefect, has the key to the door.

"I followed my procedure, checked the chest to make sure there was gold inside, together with two witnesses, my chief clerk and the Captain of the Guards. The merchant himself was a third witness. I then sealed the chest, putting my own thumbprint in the wax, and placed it on a shelf. I then locked the door to the strong room.

"Yesterday, when the merchant came to reclaim his gold, we opened the chest and found a pile of dirt. No gold, just dirt. The guards swore no one entered the strong room, so I immediately had them arrested for accepting a bribe.

"Since the seal was in place with my thumbprint in the wax, the Imperial Censor is coming to discover if I had a role in the theft.

"The gold just vanished. It became a pile of dirt."

The Prefect shook his head slowly. "I just don't understand how the gold could have been removed with my seal in place, in a locked room with the only key hanging on a chain around my neck."

"Was this merchant from this area, Prefect Wang?" Master Bao asked.

"No, he was traveling from Jiannan Province, and

was going to purchase a ship in the harbor at Lang Fu."

"Ah," Master Bao said, "and is he a gold merchant, perhaps?"

"Yes," the Prefect replied. "He is, and the Imperial Treasury will pay him for his loss. But, Master Bao, his gold disappeared from a chest sealed with my thumbprint. What could his occupation have to do with that?"

"If you would be kind enough to show me this magic box, perhaps I can help clear up the mystery."

"We can view the chest together with the Imperial Censor this very afternoon, for he will have arrived and will be at *The Inn of Harmony* in the city," Prefect Wang said. He gave another great sigh as he rose. "Thank you for listening, Master Bao, but I fear no one can help me. Soon, my head will fall on the execution grounds."

Two hours later, Master Bao, Ping, Prefect Wang and Imperial Censor Ch'ang Hao, stood around a table in the locked room. On the table was a metal chest used to convey gold.

Prefect Wang opened the chest, and revealed it was half filled with dirt.

Master Bao stepped up to the table. "Ping and I stopped on our way here to purchase a jar of gold paint from the Goldsmith's Guild. Artisans use it on certain types of metal decorations.

"Something is unusual about this chest. The bottom is lead, and there is a hidden bottom of lead beneath that. The lead gives the chest the weight that the soil alone doesn't have.

"Did you lift the chest yourself, Prefect Wang, when the merchant brought it here?"

"No. One of his servants carried the chest in, but it appeared to be quite heavy, and the servant grunted when he placed it on the table."

Ping handed Master Bao his water bag.

"Using the water from my water bag, I moisten the soil in the chest, and then I mold it into mounds the size and shape of gold bars. As you can see, the soil is still moist as I paint them gold. A man such as a gold worker would be much more adept at using this paint, but you can see they appear quite real."

"Yes," Censor Ch'ang said, "it is difficult to tell them from real gold. As they lie, they look very real."

Censor Ch'ang closed the chest. "It is time for our noon rice, and I suggest we bring the box with us. We shouldn't let it out of our sight." Prefect Wang took one handle and Censor Ch'ang took the other.

Two hours passed before the men returned to the locked room. The heavy chest was placed in the middle of the table, and the men gathered around. Before the chest was open, Censor Ch'ang spoke, "Master Bao, it is because of your reputation and the reputation of Wang that I have allowed these unusual procedures. Now, I know there are four gold-painted mounds of dirt in that box, for I have been with the chest for hours. I'm curious to see what you will do next?"

"Thank you for your trust and patience, Censor Ch'ang. Now, please open the box so we can view the contents," Master Bao said.

Censor Ch'ang threw open the lid of the box, peered inside, and jumped back. He swung to glare at Master Bao, his face becoming red.

Prefect Wang peered into the chest, stepped back, and stared at the monk, his mouth open.

There were only piles of dirt in the box. "Where did the gold paint go?" asked Prefect Wang.

Master Bao just smiled.

"How did this happen, Monk?" Censor Ch'ang demanded. "What sorcery is this that can make gold paint disappear?"

"No sorcery, Imperial Censor," Master Bao said. "This is an old swindle known in remote parts of Jiannan Province. The soil in that area is unusually acidic, and it dissolves the gold paint within four or five hours, if the soil is dry. Moisture speeds the process.

"Once I heard the merchant was from Jiannan, and a goldsmith, I suspected such a swindle. The gold did not vanish because there never was any gold."

"You have saved my life, Master Bao," Prefect Wang said. His eyes appeared moist.

"I think we should be investigating to see if there is a tie between the merchant and the tyrant Li Chia," Censor Ch'ang said. "It's likely he was behind this plot to remove you from office, Wang, because you were about to investigate his smuggling."

"I'll return to the Prefecture and begin at once," said Wang.

"And Ping and I will be stopping at the *White Cloud Daoist Monastery* for a week of contemplating the *Dao*. In each his own way, our duties are clear."

The next day, Master Bao and Ping were having tea in the *White Cloud Daoist Monastery*. Ping stood and bowed deeply to the monk, his hands clasped inside his capacious sleeves. "Please enlighten this ignorant pupil, Master," Ping said. "You turned down the Third Princess when she asked you to be an advisor to the Emperor himself, yet you helped Prefect Wang resolve a difficult situation."

"Yes, Ping. That is true."

"Isn't helping the Emperor the same as helping a Prefect, both officials in the Dragon Empire?

Master Bao smiled. "Prefect Wang is a good man who assists the people in his official capacity. He suffered a great wrong that I was able to help resolve.

"The Imperial Court is a maze of conflicting passions and plots, most of which are vastly different than my *Dao* philosophy. I would be of little use to the people of the Empire."

Ping nodded and bowed again. "So the sage must help those he can assist in righting a wrong, but still remain free from entanglements. This is the way of independence. Is that correct, Master?"

"Yes, Ping. Independence, equanimity, and kindness, are the goals of the *Followers of the Way*.

"When we encounter a wrong, we do what we can to repair the rip in the social fabric of the Empire. That is the role of the sage."

The Magistrate and the Monk

*Repairing the Torn Fabric
of the Society*

Master Bao rode his ox, Xi, along a road leading to the city of Pao-Chou in the providence of Jiannan. His student, Ping, walked alongside.

"This city has an able administrator with a reputation for clever decisions in complex cases, Ping. His name is Sun Pao, and we can learn much from such a man. Therefore, as the mid-day session of the Tribunal is about to begin, we will attend and witness the proceedings."

The Tribunal was crowded and Ping noticed how people were laughing and smiling, despite the six constables at the front of the room who were lined up in two rows, holding their leather whips and bamboo rods. The table, behind which the Magistrate was to sit, was set on a high platform and covered with a red cloth. "Justice" and "Benevolence" in gold characters were embroidered on the front of the cloth.

After a few minutes, the curtain behind the dais was pulled aside by two men dressed in bronze armor, and the Magistrate emerged. He was a large man with a long, dark beard and wore the green brocade robe of his office. A black, winged cap, the *zanjiao futou*, completed the official wardrobe.

The crowd grew silent.

After a quick survey of the room, the Magistrate wrote on a flat piece of wood and handed it to the Chief Constable. Ping knew that this would be the name of the prisoner to be brought before the bench.

Time passed and the crowd began to grow restless. "Silence," thundered the Magistrate as he pounded on the table with his gavel known as "the wood that frightens the hall."

The Chief Constable brought in not one, but two men, and made them kneel on the marble floor before the bench.

"A blind, elderly woman was attacked and robbed by one of you," the Magistrate roared. "The other man, who is a villager, gave chase and caught the robber. But the robber lied and said the villager did the crime and he was caught by the man who is really the robber.

Both of you say the other is guilty of the crime.

"As the blind woman cannot identify her attacker, we will settle this mystery another way. Constables, take the two men outside and have them run to the city gate. Bring the men back and tell me who won the footrace."

When the men were returned to the Tribunal, the Magistrate said, "The faster runner is the honest man who caught the slower robber. Now we know who is guilty and he will now confess to his heinous crime."

With one look at the constables and their instruments of torture, the slower man quickly confessed and was led back to jail.

The crowd cheered and laughed at the clever way the Magistrate had settled the case.

Later, Master Bao and Ping found a stable for Xi, and went for a walk in the crowded marketplace of Pao-Chou.

As they were looking over the vendors' stalls of various goods, a tall man dressed as a craftsman with his lower face covered by a cloth, spoke quietly to Master Bao.

"I saw you in the Tribunal today," he said, "standing at the rear of the hall."

Master Bao smiled. "And I see you are disguised, Magistrate Sun Pao, so you can circulate among the people. You'll forgive me for not bowing, for that would give your true identity away."

"And I won't bow to the revered monk, Master Bao, for the people will trouble you to heal them."

Ping was busy buying a sticky treat and took no notice of the two men speaking quietly.

Suddenly, a villager accidentally bumped into a vendor of *huan-san*, a ring-shaped rice cake. The vendor's cart tipped and several cakes fell to the ground and broke into many pieces. The villager said,"I'm sorry for the damage to your cakes. It looks like about one hundred and I will gladly pay for them."

"One hundred?" the vendor said with a snarl. "It was three hundred cakes."

The two men began to argue.

The Magistrate whispered to Master Bao. "I'll let you handle this problem, Master Bao, so I can witness your sagacity."

Master Bao smiled, and approached the two men. "Perhaps I can help," he said. "Weigh one full, undamaged cake."

"Yes, Master Monk, but I don't see what that will do," the vendor said. "This undamaged cake weighs five *kans*," he reported after putting it on a scale.

"Now, gather up the broken cakes and weigh them together," Master Bao said.

The vendor did as asked and said, "The total is five-hundred *kans*."

Master Bao bowed to the vendor, "The number of damaged cakes, therefore, is one hundred."

The Magistrate of Pao-Chou and the monk strolled away together, with Ping following behind listening to their learned conversation. All three enjoyed a pot of tea and some unbroken rice cakes at a local restaurant.

The next morning, as Master Bao and Ping were passing through the South Gate of Pao-Chou on their way to the next Province, Ping spoke up, "Master, you would make a great Magistrate. Do any monks who follow *The Way* ever go into politics and become officers of the Empire?"

"Oh yes, Student Ping. The medicine sage, Song Xiao, was a close advisor of Emperor Taizhong. He taught the emperor that body and mind are cultivated by simple living, and that the emperor's duty was to his people, not to himself. Master Song had great influence over the welfare of the citizens."

"I have not heard of Song Xiao, Master."

"That's as it should be. A *Follower of the Way* should not seek or encourage recognition for his or her works."

Master Bao was silent for a time, riding quietly on Xi. Then he turned to face Ping. "Each of us must make our own decision as to what path we choose to follow, if we are to be of service to the people of this empire.

"For example, the Immortal Luo Gongyuan is a hermit, but often advises officials who track him down in the mountains.

"I am an itinerant monk, going about the kingdom with my student, fixing the fabric of this great society when I find it torn, and when the *Will of Heaven* deems that I should do so.

"That is my role in helping the people of the Dragon Empire."

The Water Buffalo and the Dao

"Sages do not accumulate, Student Ping. The more they give to others, the more they gain."

Master Bao rode his great ox, Xi, along a river road in the district of Hue-Pen. His student, Ping, walked alongside.

"This is a wide river, Master," Ping exclaimed, "with a lot of boat traffic."

Master Bao turned to Ping. "Indeed, Student Ping," Master Bao said. "Wide and long. The Hue River stretches over a thousand Li, from Shannandong Province to the sea. The next village, Lan-Fang, is well-known as a trading port."

Just ahead, a group of six men dressed as merchants were huddled together deep in conversation. They stood on a dock to which a small boat was tied.

Also standing on the dock was a farmer holding a rope tied around the neck of a water buffalo that stood in the boat, passively chewing its cud.

One of the men looked up and saw Master Bao and Ping. "Here's a wise monk," he cried, "maybe he can help us with this problem."

Master Bao dismounted from Xi. "What seems to be the difficulty?" he asked.

"This farmer wishes to sell his water buffalo. The price is determined by the buffalo's weight. The farmer claims it weighs 1000 *talacs*. We say it weighs no more than 800 *talacs*, and will pay him for that weight. As we have no way of weighing the beast, we are at an impasse."

Master Bao looked at the water buffalo, the boat, and the pile of ballast rocks nearby.

"Put a mark on the hull of the boat at the water line while the buffalo is in the boat. Then, lead the animal off of the boat," Master Bao said.

The men did as he directed, while the farmer with the buffalo stood by and watched.

"Now, as those ballast rocks are each marked with its weight, fill the boat with ballast until the water mark of the bull in the boat is reached. Add up the weight of the ballast and you will have the weight of the water buffalo."

The merchants' servants filled the boat with the marked ballast. The men then added up the weight.

"Exactly 900 *talacs*," one of the merchants said. "And that's what we'll pay."

The farmer smiled and bowed, took his money and gave the bull's rope to one of the servants.

"Thank you, Wise Monk. You solved our problem," a merchant said as he bowed deeply.

Late that afternoon, Master Bao and Ping entered the village of Lan-fang. The flavorful odors of steamed vegetables and rice cakes from a small restaurant beckoned the travelers to their evening meal.

After eating, Ping stood and bowed deeply to Master Bao, his hands clasped inside his capacious sleeves. "Master, you solved a difficult problem for those wealthy merchants, yet none offered you a reward. No one took your name to tell other merchants how clever you were, and thereby spreading your reputation as a wise monk throughout this region. You will be forgotten, rather than famous for your wisdom."

Master Bao smiled. "Remember the teachings of the august Lao Tze, Student Ping.

> 'Sages do not accumulate
> *The more they assist others, the more they possess,*
> *The more they give to others, the more they gain.*

> 'The Dao of Heaven
> *Benefits and does not harm*
> *The Dao of Sages*
> *Assists and does not contend.'*"

Ping bowed even deeper. "Thank you, Master, for this lesson. You demonstrate that sages act without conceit, achieve without claiming credit, and do not wish to display their virtue. Truly, these are the ways of a wise sage who flows with the *Dao*."

Master Bao returned Ping's bow. "And also the ways of a wise student, Ping, for we all are in the *Flow of the Dao*, as is a fish in the flow of the river."

The Nature of the Snake and the Tiger

*"Keep fear from your heart, Ping,
and flow like water."*

Master Bao rode his great ox, Xi, along a trail through a deep forest in the southern district of Lingnan. His pupil, Ping, walked alongside.

"This jungle if full of deadly snakes, poisonous insects, and vicious tigers, Master," Ping said. "I think most travelers would avoid it."

Master Bao stopped Xi and dismounted. "The nature of the snake is to strike," he said, "just as the nature of the scorpion is to sting. The tiger hunts and kills because that is its nature. If we do not contend with these creatures, they will not harm us, as we do not have cruelty or domination in our hearts."

"I see a snake in the trail just ahead, Master. It is

a viper whose bite can kill within minutes."

Master Bao walked up to the green serpent with red eyes slithering along the side of the road. He reached down and picked the snake up, holding it in his outstretched hands.

"Know this, Student Ping. Everything in the universe is connected, interrelated. For us to become one with the *Dao*, and to avoid misfortune, we must not be separate from all of the inhabitants of this earth. The snake feels only the *Flow of the Dao* when picked up with hands as gentle as water seeping from the ground.

"Keep fear from your heart, Ping, and flow like water." He replaced the snake where he had picked it up, and watched it slip away into the roadside vegetation.

A loud roar disrupted the lesson, and a large tiger bounded onto the trail a few feet from the travelers. Xi gave a bellow and shook his great horns.

Ping stared at the tiger, who had dropped into a crouch, prepared to spring.

Master Bao stepped in front of the boy and the ox. He made a circle with his hand. "Go to your stillness inside, Ping, and the tiger will not harm us," he said, "for he will see our spirits are without material substance."

The tiger rose from its crouch and sat back on its haunches. It tipped its head to one side, then the other, looking directly at the monk, the student, and the ox.

Silence reigned in the jungle. Even the birds and insects were quiet.

With a shake of its massive head, the tiger jumped off the trail and disappeared into the thick forest. The cacophony of the jungle resumed, with bird calls and the whine of beetles. Somewhere, far away, a tiger roared.

Much later, the travelers ate their evening rice at an outside table at a small restaurant in a nearby village. After finishing their final pot of tea, and the table cleared, Ping rose and bowed deeply to Master Bao. "Today I learned of the nature of the creatures of the wild, Master. Please enlighten this ignorant pupil of the nature of my fellow men and women."

"Ah, Ping. The nature of human beings is as each of us chooses. Our nature can be kind, or it can be cruel. It can be wise, or it can be foolish. It can be peaceful, or it can be warlike.

"The scorpion's nature is to sting, and the serpent's nature is to strike. Their nature is set in stone, but humans can choose to change their nature. A cruel man can become kind, and a foolish woman can become wise.

"And in all the Universe, Student Ping, it is only a human who can choose to become a sage."

The Thief

*The fruit of a well-lived life springs
from the seeds of good conduct.*

Master Bao rode his great ox, Xi, along a tree-lined road in the kingdom of Kang in Shandong Providence. His pupil, Ping, strode alongside.

"Tonight, we will rest in the city of Hwang-Lei, Ping. It is noted for its productive rice fields, and its bountiful harvests of fruits and vegetables."

The well-traveled road soon opened to an area of vast rice fields, where many farmers worked with their oxen. Wagons pulled by still more oxen plied the road on which the monk and Ping traveled.

Soon the travelers entered the gate of the walled city of Hwang-Lei, and stopped at an inn on the main street. A wooden sign swaying slightly in the soft breeze told them it was *The Inn of the Plum Blossom Bower*.

After turning Xi over to the stable lad for a rub-down and meal, the travelers pushed open the door to the lobby of the inn. Upon entering, they noticed a commotion taking place in front of the registration counter.

A thin man dressed in rags was huddled on the floor, his hands and arms protecting his head from the rain of blows and kicks from three large men. The men were cussing loudly as their punches and kicks hit home.

Master Bao stepped up to the fracas and pushed the three sweating men aside. Recognizing the monk, the men stepped back immediately and bowed deeply to him.

"What is happening here? Why are you beating this man?"

"He is a thief, Master," the tallest one said. "We caught him stealing silver from the money box behind the counter. Rather than call the constables, which would mean the Magistrate would become involved and we would need to be witnesses, we decided to mete out justice ourselves."

Master Bao and Ping helped the victim of the beating to his feet, and brought him, limping and bent over, to a chair in the lobby. "Justice is the province of those given the *Mandate of Heaven* and the representatives of the Dragon Throne. Anger and beating this man will not change him. It will only harden your own heart with shame.

"Bring me warm water and soap," the monk ordered the innkeeper. "And fetch vinegar and plasters for this man's injuries."

Shortly after washing and treating the thief's wounds, Master Bao and Ping treated him to a meal at a nearby restaurant.

"Heaven itself is against me, Master," the man moaned while gobbling down a large bowl of noodles. "I, Ma Gan, am the unluckiest man on this planet."

After Ma Gan had eaten his fill of noodles and emptied several cups of tea, he bowed deeply to Master Bao. "Since I was but a child, people have hated me, treated me with disdain, and laughed at me, all for no reason. It is my miserable fate to have the stars lined up against me. Woe is my life…"

Master Bao and Ping listened carefully to Ma Gan's laments until he finally fell silent.

"Tell me, Ma Gan. Why did you try to steal the silver from the money box at the inn?"

"I was hungry, Master. I hadn't eaten in three days."

"Then why didn't you steal the bread that was in the kitchen in the inn's restaurant, right in the next room? You can't eat silver, and did you not know it was guarded?"

"It was my terrible luck to get caught, Master. That's all. I thought, if I steal the silver, I can have many loaves of bread, and many meals. But if I steal the bread, I'll be hungry again tomorrow."

"So you looked into the future, rather than satisfy your immediate need for food. By not remaining in the present, you received a beating."

Ma Gan was silent, his head cocked to one side. "So if I wish to become lucky, I should steal only what I need."

"Is there no work you can do so you wouldn't need to steal in order to live?"

"I have worked, Master," Ma Gan wailed, "but bad luck always seems to come my way. I was a clerk for a woolen goods store, but, because of my crossed stars, I was beaten and fired."

"What happened?"

"Curse my luck, the owner had a beautiful daughter. He caught me trying to persuade her to share her bed with me."

"So you were untrustworthy in the eyes of the owner, and he responded by beating you and throwing you from the store."

"Yes. You can see how unfortunate I have been. When I worked for a farmer, he fired me because I stole one of his goats. He had many, and I didn't think he'd miss one. It was just my ill fortune that he was a farmer who knew each of his goats by name and quickly found one missing." Here, Ma Gan burst into tears.

"Listen carefully, Ma Gan. The past and future are ghosts. Dwelling in them only bring fear and regret."

Ma Gan dried his eyes on his dirty sleeve and seemed to be listening to the monk.

Master Bao went on, speaking quietly. "Neither Heaven nor Life seek to harm you. Lay aside your mistrust of the Universe, and seek to live in the Present without fear. Accept the world as you find it, for only then can you have true peace of mind."

The monk and Ping rose to go. "Go, Ma Gan, to *The Temple of Bountiful Beauty* that is nearby. If you desire to truly change your attitude, meet with the Chief Abbot. From then on, your life will be as you choose to make it.

"Remember, inner balance and proper behavior, together with acceptance of the *Will of Heaven*, will bring you a life of well-being."

Later, after eating their evening rice, Ping approached Master Bao, bowed deeply three times with his hands fold inside his capacious sleeves, and said, "Please, Master. I heard all you told the thief, but will he follow your wisdom?"

Master Bao smiled. "That we cannot know, Student Ping. Each must find his own spiritual path, and our role was merely to point out one possible road to his inner peace.

"Master Lao Tzu said that the fruit of a well-lived life springs from the seed of good conduct. And that is keeping in the *Flow of the Dao*."

About the Author

" When just a lad, it occurred to me that life was merely a series of experiences, and I determined to have a whole bunch of those. So, I became a medical technologist, a steely-eyed Forensic Investigator, a tracker of man and beast, a wilderness skills instructor, a U.S. Navy Lieutenant, and a Police Science Instructor. Finally, I became a writer of mysteries. And I'm also a husband, father, grandfather, and great-grandfather. "

Visit Tom Hanratty at www.thomashanratty.com for a listing of his other books.

Cover & Interior Design by Kristi Ryder www.kryderdesign.com

Made in the USA
Middletown, DE
08 September 2021

47802009R10085